SISTERS
AND
STRANGERS

SISTERS
AND
STRANGERS

A Moral Tale

EMMA TENNANT

GRAFTON BOOKS

A Division of the Collins Publishing Group

LONDON GLASGOW
TORONTO SYDNEY AUCKLAND

Grafton Books
A Division of the Collins Publishing Group
8 Grafton Street, London W1X 3LA

Published by Grafton Books 1990

A CIP catalogue record for this book is available
from the British Library

ISBN 0-246-13429-1

Phototypeset by Computape (Pickering) Ltd, North Yorkshire
Printed in Great Britain by
William Collins Sons & Co. Ltd, Glasgow

For Patricia Parkin

When my friend Elsie and I were young we were taken each year to stay with her mother's mother in her house by the sea in that rocky piece of magic that is Cornwall (there was even a resident mermaid). And the stories Grandmother Dummer told us here haunted our dreams long after we were grown up and she had died.

It wasn't just that we knew Red Riding Hood would come out of the woods above Zennor – for that was where Grandmother Dummer lived, with nothing but a tin-miners' pub and an old church with that sea-maiden's face, unforgettably, engraved on a stone slab inside, for company. It was, quite simply, that we saw her.

The red cape, and the hood with its trimming of white fur, would flash in and out of the trees on the sunny days we walked through the wood to the sea.

The frog that jumped away in long grass came to our pillow at night.

Dressed as princesses, we played with him in our palace and prayed for the morning when he would turn into a handsome young man.

Sometimes, walking in our sleep on dark and starless nights along the coastal path to the furthest tip of the land, we came to the thorny thicket where the prince lay sleeping; but we could never get through the bramble to wake him with a kiss.

– It's just as well, Elsie's mother's mother would say. You don't know enough yet. Life's not all fairy stories, you know.

But we knew it was. Some of the stories had happy endings and others were sad and cruel.

We had no way of knowing how ours would go.

At last, Grandma became impatient with us.

– There are seven ways, she said. And nothing's changed since the very first woman was plucked from Adam's rib-cage. Seven ways and seven women, and you'll be all of them in your time. But you'll never love each other, unless you learn to become one.

We didn't know what she meant, of course. Who are these seven women, we said? Again and again, because our dreams were filled now with these women, walking in avenues of fine coral, beneath the sea.

– Very well, Elsie's Grandmother Dummer said. But don't blame me if you don't understand a fairy story for grown-ups.

And she made us sit either side of her, on the low sill of her old house, with the window that looks out across a short stretch of heath to a dark blue – or an angry grey – or a midnight sea, and she said: Very well, then. So. I'll start with the story of ...

EVE

There once was a woman who was so ridiculously happy that she hardly dared to go out into the world.

She had found love, you see.

And she knew that all the sad, bitter women out there would stab her with their glances of envy and reproach.

If she went to a supermarket, she would be handed an apple that was red one side and green the other, and as she bit into it she would die.

If she went to a party – and she had to sometimes, because of her husband's work – her dress would turn to tatters at midnight and the car on the way home would lose its wheels and roll as helpless as a pumpkin to certain death.

And if she had a best woman friend (God forbid!), that friend would seize a wand from the *batterie de cuisine* that Eve kept so gleaming in her brand-new kitchen and turn her into a little mouse or a shrew.

So Eve was very careful.

*

She was careful of her beauty, too. Eve wore night creams of almonds and day creams of powdered rhinoceros horn and she rubbed the tails of embryo sea-horses on her eyebrows so they shone and bristled like a film-star's.

Eve cleaned her teeth with ground river pearls, gathered from freshwater mussels in the river at Beaulieu where it runs beneath the romantic island fortress of Eilean Aigus.

And she washed her hair with seaweed drawn from the ocean bed on the most westerly coast of Bequia, where the voodoo magic says that it must be gathered at the crowing of the white cock.

After her bath, while waiting for the key in the door, the moment of Adam's return from another busy day as managing director of a multimedia corporation, Eve rubbed oils of Afghan pansies and unguents made from samphire buds found on the highest cliffs of County Kerry into her pale skin.

Her nails she painted with liquid silver dust, refined at the time of the new moon in her own enchanting garden.

– But where does Eve live?

Grandmother Dummer laughed at us when we asked that.

– My dears, she said (for children are practical, really, and their fairy stories must have all the trappings of circumstantial evidence), my dears, Eve is everywhere. She's down the road, just before the turning where the bus stops for Penzance, Grandmother Dummer said. The house with the walled garden ... surely you remember, girls, when you tried to climb up and get the pears?

Elsie and I looked at each other. When we were at school,

leading the kind of humdrum life expected of us (of course we'd spin tales of it when we were old, remember those days as if they were a fairy tale and quite different from the way they really were), it never occurred to us that women like Eve could be living – just like that, right amongst us and we had no idea of it at all.

So we decided that the house we'd glimpsed when we scaled the wall by the crossroads of the Zennor-Penzance road must be Eve's true home.

It was a bit like deciding Father Christmas had just one address in Lapland, I suppose. The fact that there were an infinite number of him didn't make him any less real, for all that.

– So what did Eve *do* all day? we asked when Grand-mother Dummer fell silent and sat staring out at the falling dusk as if it would wipe out her memory altogether. Please, Elsie added – for this was her grandmother, after all, and a very special one, with a direct line to a mermaid in the tiny church – you could hear her sing from your bedroom window on nights when the sea was getting up ...

Grandmother Dummer said it wasn't so much a question of what Eve did, it was what she didn't do.

– It's not a story of an olden-days princess, Grandmother Dummer said. She's here and now. And one day, mark my words, you may turn out exactly like her.

Then it was our turn to laugh; but Grandmother Dummer shushed us and went on.

– Eve has had dinner ready for as long as it's been in the specially prepared freeze-heater, replenished at the Manoir

Au Quat' Saisons each week by the master chef Raymond Blanc, and containing an exact balance of protein and calorie and stimulant and gentle narcotic – lettuce soup, most probably. Adam will come in to a hall mirrored and laid to Spanish tiles, hidden from the world by ruched blinds of silk from Chiang Mai; and further on, in the elegant drawing-room, muffling his tread – for he's in a hurry to see his Eve, to hold her in his arms again and tell her how much he loves her …

– Yes? For Grandmother Dummer has fallen silent again. It was the first time, perhaps, that we guessed the power and sadness of love; and how even an old woman will feel lonely and unhappy at the thought of the bliss of Eve.

– Yes, said Grandmother Dummer. As I was saying, Adam's feet are sinking into carpets from Bessarabia and rag rugs from the souks of Fez, his hand is going to a glass of Waterford crystal for his evening slug of Scotch.

Well, poor man, he needs it after such a day of global and interstellar decisions the multi-mega-media business now demands.

And – don't forget I told you this story wasn't suitable for you at all – Eve is waiting for him in her boudoir specially built for her at the top of the house.

Eve lies on a bed that is an exact replica of Cleopatra's barge, in a peignoir of seven thousand, seven hundred and seventy-seven rose petals, each petal strengthened with gold thread spun by the Lulworth royal silkworms and each petal taken from the roses Aurore and Albertine that grow in Eve's beautiful rose garden.

She smells of musk and raspberry juice, and a faint sprinkling of Floris's Oriental bouquet on bed and cushions gives the room an opulent, exotic air.

Eve's eyelids are half-moons of Persian violet; and everywhere she looks she sees her favourite colour.

Mauve.

A fleshy mauve, like an orchid.

Adam has come in, and, pulling her peignoir away from her ...

— But there, my children, I must break off.

— And, said Grandmother Dummer when we looked up at her imploringly, it didn't happen anyway. Because something had taken place that day which was to change the course of this happy couple's life.

It had to do with a simple question of matrimony. As it so often does.

— You don't know yet, said Grandmother Dummer. But the Paradise I've been describing can't exist for very long.

It's one of the basic tenets of life. Nature abhors a vacuum. And what is more of a vacuum than perfection?

There's nothing more lovely, of course, she went on hurriedly, than a happy life and a beautiful garden and a dream house ... and being in love ...

But it just isn't allowed, so you'll have to believe me.

Eve didn't know that, of course. She had to learn the hard way. And the strange thing is, Eve still doesn't know today.

She can't understand that it's true: that if everything's perfect, sure as anything it'll be taken away from you.

So, on that idyllic summer evening when Adam comes back to his love nest, and walks up the ivory staircase inlaid with mother-of-pearl (Adam is very, very rich), there have already been the first stirrings of something-not-quite-right in the palace of dreams.

It's as if a door were open somewhere, sending a draught down the spine and turning beauties into red-nosed snifflers just like that. Like the first signs of the north wind, when it blows down from the polar wastes and the flowers shrivel and go blind. But Eve was prepared for a frosty winter, with a blazing log fire in the Moroccan pavilion they had transported from Taroudant, and the thick furs of Siberian fox to keep them warm as they make love in front of the flames. Great silver thermoses of hot soup – minestrone and cock-a-leekie and mutton soup with barley – had been planned by Eve, recipes noted on the computer for easy access; haggis ordered for the cruellest of the winter months, radishes and anchovies and oysters with tabasco, all the spiciest things as love-aides in the weeks of Lent.

But oh dear no, said Grandmother Dummer. It wasn't going to be like that at all.

Did we see a glimmer of enjoyment in Grandmother Dummer's eyes? Surely she *wanted* Eve and Adam to be happy?

Didn't she?

Or was it just that going against the shape of the story, bending the tale of life, as it were, is simply wrong?

Eve had to learn the hard way.

But we, of course, wanted her to go on like that for ever.

– The first chill, Grandmother Dummer said, came on that very day I was telling you of.

Adam came back from work more in love than ever. As he climbed the stairs he slipped the gift-wrapped box that had been in his pocket into his left hand.

I won't tell you what the gift was. Just think what you'd most like in the world – and that's what Adam gave Eve. Every day.

And she was always delighted as if it were the first time in her life anyone had given her anything.

Adam paused on the landing to turn on the fountains in the Sky Conservatory.

When the fountains played, illumined by trapped sunlight (it was really nuclear power, but Adam didn't like to say this to Eve), the glass ceiling of Eve's boudoir swelled with golden globules of water and light. Making love became, as their lips met and then their eager bodies, like copulating with the Universe, both under an ocean and floating through space.

So – Adam turns on the fountains.

He advances on Eve. The heart of the rose, in her thousands upon thousands of petals, the slender stamen of the neck, the eyelids like the wings of a Laotian moth.

The eyelids flutter slightly. Two sapphire orbs, whites as clear as snow from eye baths of gentian and camomile mixed with a secret ingredient from the burnt-out palace of the greedy Empress of the Philippines, become visible, as Eve pretends to wake up.

Adam knows Eve hasn't been asleep, and his one great joy is to pretend to have difficulty in waking her.

So – gift outstretched – Adam advances on the Barge Bed and kneels by the golden prow to coax his sweetheart awake.

Eve's mouth opens at the same time as her eyes.

The voice that comes out is unfamiliar to Adam. (He even wonders for a moment if Eve has been practising ventriloquism, along with her classes in Batik and Provençal pottery and the occasional fencing and martial arts.)

– A woman came to the house today, Eve says.

She says she's your wife.

THE FLY IN
THE OINTMENT

It is true that Eve had been careful (as she always was, wasn't she, not to worry her man when he was tired from the office, to keep him and lie by him if not stand by him – here comes her chance) – had been careful, as I say, not to mention to Adam the strange things she seemed to have been seeing lately.

Little things. Nothing really.

It was just that every time Eve went into the kitchen to prepare herself a snack – blinis on days when there was a refreshing nip in the air; passion fruit and kiwi sorbet with mountain honey wafers when it was warm: for in the climate of love the temperature is always balmy and kind (requited love, that is) – she saw out of the corner of her eye a face by the window.

The window with the slatted blinds, the window that opens on to the street.

– Yes, Grandmother Dummer said. There is a street outside Eve's house.

However much she would like there not to be; to be enclosed forever in the demesne of her lover's private park; to grow straight from the recumbent body of Adam, a twig, a rib shooting high and bursting into leaf at the sheer joy of feeding off the income and life of Adam; however much Eve wants this, children, she will always find there is a strip of asphalt, and a pavement the dogs have fouled, and a car that makes a noise when it starts up on frosty mornings. All just bang outside Eve's house.

Don't think she and Adam hadn't done all they could to pretend the street wasn't there.

The slatted blind is of steel and when you pull the cord, all the flaps close and fit together so tight you'd think from the outside that all the gold of Fort Knox was stored inside.

And, of course, it is.

Adam believes that Eve is worth a good deal more than her weight in gold.

In fact, she is priceless to him.

But you can't live by artificial light alone. When Eve comes into the kitchen to fix a snack, which she will take to eat either in the conservatory (where her carnivorous jungle lilies turn hungrily to her as she eats) or to the garden where the south wall has nectarines and peaches for the picking, and chilled wine from the heart of the Muscat grape in a garden fridge disguised as a toadstool, she likes to feel the warm sun from the window on her back.

Eve doesn't like one moment of coldness while Adam is away. He warms her at night, so she dreams she's in a pirogue, floating the thick muddy waters of the Mekong river, idling under gold temples where the Buddha squats naked in the sun.

She doesn't want to stand under neon lights in the kitchen as she prepares her fastidious morsels.

The lighting is polar. So, more and more recently, she has taken to pulling that cord by the steel blind and letting in a zebra skin of light from the place she has quite forgotten about, the outside world.

And, of recent mornings, a face – or just a segment of it – has been appearing between the slats.

The disconcerting thing is that different parts of the face appear at different levels.

So Eve has a picture of an impossible monster in a fairy tale book. Two burning dark eyes. And then a great big mouth like an ogre's, that wants to come in and eat her and her house all up ...

◆

Elsie and I were both frightened at this and Grandmother Dummer must have noticed, for she patted us on the hand and said:

– You mustn't imagine, my dears, that things are so different for grown-ups.

Eve was just as frightened as you would be, on seeing the ogre looking in through the window.

But she is more cunning than you would be. She thought that if she said nothing to Adam and made a deal with the ogre, it would decide to go away. She couldn't tell the truth, you see. So let's hope you don't find out you've grown up to be like her.

– Why can't she tell the truth? we both wanted to know (although of course we wanted to know what the deal was that Eve made with the monster).

– Because she had decided not to take responsibility for herself, Grandmother Dummer said. She let someone else look after all the bills and the time when the rain came through the roof and the rude man from the insurance. And when you let other people take over things for you, you aren't real any more, and people who aren't real can't tell the truth.

– I see, we said. (We weren't sure we did. Eve's life sounded pretty OK, except for the fact she didn't climb trees – and she could have done that if she'd wanted, as there were bound to be plenty in her garden.)

– So what was the deal with the ogre? we said, feeling secretly sorry for Eve.

– Well, first of all she spoke through the slats and asked the monster what it wanted.

There was no answer – but, much worse, there was a terrible rush of wind and a squall of sleet that battered on the roof of the conservatory and broke several panes and it grew all of a sudden dark.

Eve didn't like this at all, as you can imagine.

She was glad, in fact, of the artificial lighting, for without it she wouldn't have been able to run out of the kitchen as quickly as she did.

Of course, she said nothing to Adam that night. He asked how his poor darling was, after the freak storm that had hit the house. And he said she wasn't to worry her pretty little head about the conservatory roof. He had already fixed up to have it mended while she was having a tennis lesson on the private courts at the end of the garden.

– Never you mind, Adam said.

And of course, the first time, they didn't.

Adam had the hailstone the size of an egg freeze-dried and mounted in gold on an ormolu stand, as a memento of Eve's incredible bravery.

The flesh-eating orchids in the conservatory, however, took a grimmer view of things and drooped considerably until the glass was mended and the thermostat turned up. It was as if, Eve often thought later, they had been the first to know of the troubles ahead.

Insects were sacrificed to them daily; and they sensed somehow that Eve would have to sacrifice a good deal to this new visitor – who (alas!) showed no sign of going away.

Eve was a bit stingy at first with her sacrifices. (That's what doing a deal is, after all: you give up as little as possible in return for what you want.)

And although Eve wanted the monster to go away very badly indeed, she reassured herself that the steel blind was after all impossible to break through – and that the computer lock, which didn't have a key that anyone might steal and copy, was totally uncrackable as no one would ever be able to guess the combination (Adam's birthday and Eve's bust measurement combined).

So, when, on one of the rare cloudy days, Eve was making herself a pepper-salami sandwich at the kitchen bar and dreaming over the Italian holiday brochure that had arrived in the morning's post, and the monster's big eyes appeared between the slats of the blind, Eve went over and quite sensibly asked it if it would like some of the mango ice-cream she kept in the freezer for refreshment after a particularly tropical bout of lovemaking with Adam in the Caribbean waterbed in the garden beach-house. Maybe, Eve thought, the monster is simply lonely and starved of affection; and I have so much after all. Just one scoop of mango would hardly go missing.

(For Adam, surprisingly, given all his generosity, was an extremely careful and cheeseparing home economist. Even the proverbial pieces of string too short to be of any use were glued together by Filipino servants in the staff quarters that Eve was never allowed to visit, and used for staking plants in the garden, and the like.)

So Eve was risking quite a bit when she took the scoop of yellow, love-perfumed fruit ice-cream over to the slatted blind.

Adam might wonder why she had wanted some, all alone in the house all day. Did she have a lover? The thought was too silly to be entertained, of course. But, don't forget, Eve has been very careful up to now, and if the monster hadn't come all the rest wouldn't have happened.

Or so she likes to think.

The monster stuck its tongue through the slat and took a lick of the mango.

Then – bang! A thunder clap so loud the house seemed literally to rock on its foundations.

The parakeets in the aviary designed by Lord Snowdon screamed and the puma in the tent brought from the deserts of Persia after the performance of Ted Hughes' *Orghast* to a select audience – directed by Peter Brook – burst from its cage and bounded towards the kitchen. (For a long time the puma had fancied Eve for itself: she is, after all, a tasty morsel.)

Eve joined in the screaming. The sky is so dark, it must surely be the end of the world. For a wild moment she thinks that, somewhere, Christ must be being crucified.

But that wouldn't be possible, children. Because Eve comes a long time before Jesus. Indeed, everything in the world is her fault, and poor Jesus had to die to atone for her terrible wickedness.

– But what did she do? Elsie asked. We both decided that, despite access to unlimited supplies of ice-cream, we'd rather not be Eve.

– She just *was*, Grandmother Dummer said. That was enough. And she was too inquisitive, of course. She should have known not to ask questions.

But, because any natural disaster was by now connected in her brain with the unwelcome visits of the monster, she leant right up against her fortified Venetian blind and she said – yes, she had the temerity to say:

– Who are you? And what do you want?

The thunder stopped for a moment and a thin ray of sunlight came down on the battered and tear-stained house that was the love haven of Adam and Eve.

– I'm Adam's wife, the monster said. And I need a holiday.

After which the thunder started to rumble again, in a warning, definitely menacing way.

*

As you may well imagine, Eve didn't know what to make of this. Her emotions went through the hues of a rainbow, from the indigo of anger to the green of rage and envy and the yellow of despair.

What is Eve to do? She wants to confront Adam; she wants to flee this horrible house where she has been so unhappy (it doesn't take Eve long to register a change of script); and at the same time she wants to lie in Adam's arms surrounded by her special colour, mauvey pink, which is missing from the horrible new spectrum that has opened up inside her.

The prime necessity, of course, is to get rid of the monster.

But how?

Of course it doesn't take long for Eve to realize that the monster has already given her the means of gaining at least a temporary respite from its attentions.

I'll do it by credit card, Eve says. And she goes straight to Adam's study and comes back with his Gold Card that he keeps there for further expenditure on his love nest; and, of course, for presents for Eve.

– Where do you want to go? Eve says in a more confident, almost bossy voice (she used to be a secretary before she met Adam. Would you catch her going back to work and fighting for equal opportunities, whatever – as she thinks – they may be? Certainly not).

– Italy, the monster says through the grille, as if it's an ordinary bank and Eve is cashing it a cheque. Venice and then maybe the Abruzzi.

*

Eve lifts the ivory phone shaped like an arum lily and with a mouthpiece picked out in rubies in the form of Mae West's lips. And she orders the ticket, to be collected at the airport.

– A fortnight will do, the monster says. Then I'll be back.

And, as Eve's heart sinks at the news that she'll only have fifteen days of pure bliss before it all starts up again, the sun comes out properly and a gentle breeze wafts the scent of camellias and gardenia, and the puma, hungrily prowling in the garden beyond the plate-glass window of the kitchen, strolls back to its cage and lies down in contentment, the self-locking gate closing behind it.

With both beasts out of the way, Eve runs to her master jacuzzi to allow the information she has just received to sink in. Algae and the baby shoots of sphagnum moss rise in a green cloud as she presses the jet and submerges.

Whatever is she going to do?

And – how dare Adam be married and never have told her?

For marriage was always on the tip of their tongue ... and yet – as if fearing the staleness of familiarity, the bonds that make a duty of pleasure and thus kill it – they'd always let their tongues meet in another heavenly kiss rather than say the actual words.

The house and the expensive real estate surrounding it were in Eve's name – so Adam had told her.

So she's always felt safe, protected by bricks and mortar and land – and, most important of all, the curve of Adam's arms, holding her to that very part of his anatomy from which she sprang.

Silly Eve.

– Anyway, Grandmother Dummer said with a sigh, almost as if she'd known this situation herself and it was painful to remember it, it's nearly your bedtime.

– But did the monster go to Italy? we said. And how could Adam be married to a monster, anyway?

Grandmother Dummer sighed again.

– It's only too easy, my dear. As you shall see.

Yes, the monster went to Venice, where the Grand Canal rose to its highest ever level and the Piazza San Marco was under ten feet of water and only the upper floors of the Accademia escaped such severe flooding that the beautiful pictures went unharmed.

This was the kind of thing that happened wherever the monster went, as you shall see.

Meanwhile, Eve is brooding in the bath. Who are you, and what do you want? – her own words – keep ringing in her head. And: I'm Mrs Adam First, says the voice on the far side of the blind. (Yes, Adam First is his name all right: he's the first man and Eve thought she was the first woman.)

Not now.

As Eve lies there, feeling the herbal spa jet right up into her beautiful vagina – the phone makes its marine mating call. (In the bathroom the receiver is a dolphin and the mouthpiece is set in coral. Natch.)

– Hello, Eve says in a dreamy voice. She presses the switch that shows her caller on a giant screen at the end of the tub. And she frowns when she sees it's a boring, middle-aged man sitting at a desk in an office just like any boring middle-aged man. It could have been the golden Adam, after all.

— Is that Mrs Adam First, says the man into his handset.

Eve feels her very first pang of fear and jealousy. Often she uses the name — who wouldn't? — and Adam smiles lovingly at her when she does. It's handy for the five-star hotels. And, anyway, it's easier than saying Arkadny-Trinkkheim-Arbutu, which is Eve's actual name — for no one has yet completely been able to decide whether Eve springs from the heart of Africa, or the Middle East, or even somewhere peculiar like Romania.

— Yes it is, Eve says with an attempt at that tone of confidence she has grown used to adopting with bank managers and other menials.

— We have a problem here with your Trex Star Gold Card, Mrs First. I believe your husband may have neglected to tell you that this particular facility has been transferred away from us and into the company. Thus, regretfully, rendering this card invalid.

— Oh, I see, Eve says faintly.

— Of course, we will make resources available to Mr First to cover your Italian trip, says the middle-aged man, who has suddenly become a very great deal less boring.

— And we will be informing Mr First directly that we are glad to offer these facilities, the man went on. He began to replace the handset of his phone.

— Wait! Eve's voice was a strangled shriek; then, with effort, it turned breathy and husky, as if an entire candy floss had somehow got stuck somewhere down there.

— Mr Brown? (Eve had seen his name on a neat card on the

desk. She had also seen the customer video screen just next to him on the inter-office phone system.)

Eve pressed the other switch. A slight smile spread over her face as she saw Mr Brown's expression of astonishment at the picture that was coming up on his video.

– Mrs First, the credit controller gasped. Mrs F ...

– Eve, Eve said in the same lazy voice. And she de-circulated the spa so that her lovely body lay there in the water for him to see.

◆

– Was she like the mermaid? we said when Grandmother had fallen silent again.

– Well in a way, said Grandmother Dummer. She sounded unhappy at the turn things were taking.

But mermaids have tails, as you know. And Eve hasn't.

– Oh, we said.

– So, Grandmother Dummer said hurriedly, Mr Brown agreed to wait a few days before advising Adam of the charge to his card.

– But why? we asked in unison.

– Well, Eve said she'd been rather a naughty girl and she was sure Mr Brown would understand, said Grandmother Dummer.

– How nice of Mr Brown, I said. Elsie, who is more of a budding cynic, looked thoughtful.

Mr Brown said he'd like to see Eve again.

At the same time each day. In the jacuzzi, to be precise.

– On video? we said.

– Oh no, not on video, Grandmother Dummer said, pursing her lips and looking away before telling us it was time for bed.

MEET THE SERPENT

As you can see, Grandmother Dummer said the next day, when we had gone on a blackberrying trip in the lanes and wound up in the little granite church, with its stained glass window of the saints and its stone relief of the mermaid, smiling out at us from a time unimaginably long before the coming of Christianity – As you can see, Eve has now got herself in a pretty pickle.

And you can't blame her for blurting it all out to Adam.

Especially as he'd found out about the trip to Italy all by himself.

– How did he do that? we asked. It seemed unfair on poor Eve that she was going to have to bear the blame for someone's earlier marriage: after all, it wasn't her fault that Adam married a monster before he knew her, was it?

– Oh yes, said Grandmother Dummer. It's her fault and she knows it. It's the price she pays for being Eve.

And, worst of all, as she notices on the morning of this terrible day, something is happening to her – to her looks, I mean.

Standing in the upper bathroom, which is modelled on the saloon bar in the *Titanic*, with sea-stained cabin trunks and a tape of 'Abide with Me' piping softly from behind the mahogany-throne WC, Eve sees her face in the barnacle-encrusted mirror look back at her in a strange way.

In fact, for a whole fifteen seconds – about the time it took for the fated ship to hit the iceberg – Eve doesn't recognize herself at all.

She could swear – but thank goodness, there are Adam's steps on the stairs and the soft thud of today's gift, wrapped as always in hand-printed Florentine paper and tied with gold string woven from Byzantine icon dust, as it lands on the floor outside the upper bathroom –

She could swear, as I say, that someone else altogether stared back at her from the glass.

And it was the monster.

– Oh no, we said.

– Yes. No wonder Eve begins to believe that things are her fault.

So, when Adam, whose hobby is chasing computer-hackers and employing the most expensive physicians in the world to trace viruses in his multi-million software corpus – and who has come across the strange charge on the superannuated Tritrex Gold – reaches the bedroom (Eve has by now slipped from the first-class cabin porthole, in her rose peignoir, to the Gilded Barge), he says:

– What a funny little person my Eve is, to be sure. A trip to Venice. And all on her own. Now, isn't that the very last thing I expected to come across? Eh? And without your precious Adam. Eh?

– The truth was, children, that Adam had been made immensely horny by the discovery of the charge on his credit card.

All the way home, in his re-vamped Thunderbird from the Elvis collection, he had whistled to himself in astonishment; and several times, when it was completely unnecessary, he had punched the siren that had been the property of Al Capone.

It was the first time Eve had gone behind his back and spent his money without asking him.

It was the first time, too, that Eve had shown any desire to escape from the cage where she was as happy as a lark and as sweet-voiced as a nightingale.

Obviously, Adam jumped to one conclusion only.

Eve had a lover. She was planning to meet him in Venice, where they would lie entwined in each other's arms as the water lapped the gondolas outside the window and Eve's multiple orgasms matched the cries of the gondolieri peddling their wares.

Grandmother Dummer frowned and shook her head.

– I'm not supposed to tell you these things, children. But, just as grandmothers aren't supposed to know anything about sex, nor are children; and of course we all do really. It's just a selfish plot by the people in between, and all in order to keep power, because those ignorant of sex are powerless.

*

33

– So, Grandmother Dummer said, by the time Adam purred up the drive of his mansion, jealousy had given him an absolutely enormous hard-on.

In his haste to seize Eve and ravish her, he almost forgot his present, which today was a new addition to their private zoo. (Like so many lovers, Adam and Eve played out fantasies of belonging to the animal kingdom, squirrels and bears and rabbits, and sometimes, if the moon was full and Eve was expecting her period, puma and its prey.)

The present, coiled in its glossy gift box from Fortnum & Mason, was a python.

Adam had had a reptiliary built at the far end of the garden, but he'd refused to tell Eve the purpose of the serpentine glass construction, with its jungle bogland inside and a decaying goat carcass staked out.

Anyway, he didn't forget the present after all, and by the time he'd raced up the crystal and Portuguese silver spiral staircase to the bedchamber, the python had woken in its box and was beginning to uncoil angrily.

– So we want to leave our Adam, do we?

(I know he's saying the same thing again and again. But people suffering from jealousy do nothing else.)

And Adam has pinned Eve to the floor of the barge with unaccustomed violence. It's rape, really. Not the kind of lovemaking to which Eve is accustomed.

But what can Eve do?

She remembers that dark face in the mirror and shudders.

Her mind races all the same. Adam, temporarily sated,

lies back beside her on the pillows of Mantua velvet. Now, Eve instinctively knows, is the time to do something – and there's not a moment to lose.

So Eve tells Adam that a woman has been to the house. She says she's Adam's wife. She insisted, on pain of causing grievous harm to Eve and to the house, on a holiday in Italy.

What could Eve do? After all, she says sweetly, I booked the ticket in her name – Mrs Adam First.

– Children, I shall skip the scene of Adam's contrition because we must move on to the serpent and its all-important role in our story. But you can imagine how he prayed to be forgiven; and offered to buy Eve an island in the Sporades all to herself; and threatened instant extinction to the monster who had come to the house and frightened his sweet darling.

– But why didn't you tell me you'd been married before? Eve says.

Now the scene of renunciation of the past.

'Lil has been so far from my mind that I completely forgot I'd ever been married.'

No, that won't quite do. A man who runs SatelHaven Inc. and all its subordinate companies can hardly be suffering from such a pronounced memory lapse.

'I didn't want to upset you, Eve darling.'

Well ... not much good either. Anyway Eve *is* upset now; and what is Adam going to do about it?

*

35

– And here, said Grandmother Dummer, comes the most profound silence.

As Eve lies beside him in the simulated Nilotic landscape of their pyramid bedroom, the silence grows longer and deeper all the time.

Adam could be a mummy, swathed in the bandages of the ancient past; mute and inanimate.

– Why, what should he have said? we ask.

– He should have offered to divorce his wife, Grandmother Dummer replies. Lil, Lilith, Li'l Abe's future step-mother – but I mustn't give the game away – must absolutely be known as the first Mrs First.

– Why won't he? we ask again.

– My dears, Adam is terrified of Lil.

For all his valour, for all his shining armour and his fleet of racing cars – hydro-adaptive, of course, and thus able to cross from Dover to Calais in 3.5 minutes – Adam cannot slay the dragon when it comes to it.

And Eve suddenly sees this.

She also sees that Adam has a cruel, insensitive streak (think of that near-rape – *really*) and that if he decided to throw Eve over – for another secretary at the office, or a beautiful stewardess on his private plane, somewhere over Borneo – Eve might lose out very badly indeed. Who says it's true that the house and land are in her name? And, even if they are, they certainly don't amount to fifty per cent of Adam's holdings. She is his true wife. They must marry.

Adam, as he lies in that eternal silence, thinks of all the

money that would go to Lil, the monster, the ravening wolf who would eat his shares in Consolidated Gold and swallow whole emerald mines in South Africa and freeze the water companies Adam has just invested in so that nothing but a spurt of dirt would gush from householders' taps.

He sees Lil the wolf and vampire, blowing down the lovely house where he lives with Eve, and gloating in the ruins while the puma, freed by her gust of breath, roams the countryside, killing and terrifying innocent people.

Adam's medal, for services to the poor and deserving, will be stripped from his chest, when it is made known that this force of destruction is actually, still, his wife.

So Adam says nothing.

Eve, idly toying with the gift-wrapped box, has opened the Piranesi-engraved wrapping and lifted the lid to look down at the coiling python.

As she screams – and the serpent lifts its head and shows a forked tongue and gives a hiss that drowns out the Mommas and the Poppas on octo-stereo – the doorbell rings.

– This may sound quite a run-of-the-mill thing to you, children. But in Adam and Eve's house, although a bell was of course installed – with flute notes, ending on a French hunting call – this is the first time that anyone has actually rung it. (Tradesmen and the like go to a separate block, screened by ilex and magnolia.)

Adam speaks into the remote-control receiver.

– Well I'm blowed, he says when he has heard a voice

37

crackle down it. It's old Frank Blake, used to be my mate at school. He's been up the Orinoco and I haven't seen him for years.

– Ask him in, Eve says, relieved. For the flute music appears to have calmed the snake and it has settled down in its box again. I'd love to meet your best friend, Eve says with a winning smile, and replaces the serpent in the box before pulling her peignoir round her and going to greet another.

THE TEMPTATION
OF EVE

Frank Blake was the kind of man who's just cut out to be a best friend. Of the family. Of Adam. Of Adam and Eve together. It doesn't matter about the combination. Frank Blake will fit in perfectly, carrying tea out on the lawn when Eve is too tired, or playing backgammon until late with Adam if the couple need a rest from each other.

Not that Adam and Eve had any need to be apart: indeed, they could hardly wait, as we have seen, to fall into each other's arms at the end of the day.

Until today, that is.

Even if Adam is contrite – and so he should be, letting a horrible old wife prowl round the grounds and frighten his sweetheart almost to death – the very fact of a serious issue having been raised has made him grumpy and off-hand.

Adam suddenly remembers that he never set up the steam train set, a complete Orient Express in its own shed at the end of the garden, and that the signals need rewiring.

Frank Blake, of course, needs no prompting. He understands everything about train sets, even complicated ones with points and junction boxes. And he knows how to mend the miniature lights which are stuck at green.

In order to avoid a future collision, Adam and Frank Blake go off to the train shed, which is a faithful replica of the Gare Saint-Lazare. And Eve is left feeling, for the first time, that it's not just a toy collision the men are determined to avoid.

Why?

Eve begins to panic. Is she losing her looks? Why was it that Adam's gait, as he strode towards the train terminal, was so like that of a man planning to go off on a real journey?

Eve has that unpleasant sensation of a once-secure landscape slipping away from under her feet.

She doesn't dare go and look in the mirror in case the monster is back.

She needs a friend, a confidant, someone to help her in this new phase of her relationship with Adam.

And who better than the charming, helpful Frank Blake?

◆

So, when the magic evening hour has come and the servants have cleared the last of the Sangria and left *doppio gliko* Greek coffee and a tray of wafer-thin praline sticks with mint-and-frosted-sugar-coating on the low table between them, Eve turns to Frank with her most seductive smile.

Adam has gone off to 'see to' the pike in the ornamental pond, another male pursuit which hasn't taken up any of his time in the past. Nor is it clear in what way the pike need seeing to; unless a visit to the Trappist monastery installed by Adam – and of which the pond forms an outlet from the replica twelfth-century moat – is really his intention.

In silence, Adam may wish to drown his sorrows with a few glasses of the mauve chartreuse made by the monks to a secret recipe and tinted with the fragrant petals of campion to the favourite colour of the mistress of the Garden of Eden.

Whichever it is, Eve has seized the opportunity to don her most lovely robe. Spun from the wings of sapphire moths, each eye jewelled with a cabochon-cut emerald, the dress seems like a night sky alive with the probing eyes of love.

And Eve is desperate for help.

Not once has Adam glanced at her in the course of the whole evening. The crayfish-catching ceremony for hors d'oeuvres, which used to afford them so much simple pleasure – running barefoot in the chalk stream in the garden and tossing the catch to the waiting chef, ready at the water's side with wok and outdoor barbecue, so that the heavenly smell of ginger and spring onion wafts to the skies in a melody of East and West combined – had Adam stomping angrily in the shallows with his trousers turned up and complaining loudly at the coldness of the water. Only Frank Blake, Eve reflected sadly, had really enjoyed himself.

Then the sucking pig, turning on its spit to the accompaniment of a shower of fresh-minted sovereigns spilling from its gaping mouth, had failed to have Adam in fits of laughter, as it normally did.

The soufflé of white truffles had even failed to rise tonight and Adam had complained about it being a waste of money.

So –

– What can I do for you my dear? (Frank Blake was intuitive. Women like that. Certainly Eve felt she had never met a better friend in her life.)

Eve told him about the monster, and the credit card and the trip to Italy. Everything except pressing the button in the jacuzzi and playing Susannah and the Elders when she should have stuck with being Eve.

– It's perfectly clear, Frank Blake said.

And he said it was obvious to him that Adam was pining for a family and he didn't know how to say so.

– Adam will love you so much if you give him a child, Frank Blake said. Just think of the joy for the child, to be brought up in such a lovely home. And by such wonderful parents, the Serpent added unctuously.

For there was no doubt in Eve's mind – whether she had drunk too much of the brandy last consumed at the Battle of Magenta by Napoleon, or had too little sleep for her afternoon rest, after Adam's mauling – that Frank Blake seemed to have turned in front of her eyes into a polite, balding, super-sleek snake.

– You think I'd make a good enough mother? says poor Eve.

– Perfection, says the python, who is now swaying dangerously in his basket chair as if inaudible harmonies are moving him in his wicked ways.

– Now, said Grandmother Dummer. I'll explain why the Serpent shouldn't have tempted Eve with the idea of having a child.

In the old days, you see, sex was the original sin.

And Eve's eating of an apple from the tree of the knowledge of good and evil meant that she would lead Adam away from a state of innocence and so start a tainted, wicked race.

But thousands and thousands of years have passed since then.

God is still there all right, but Mammon has become his chief plenipotentiary. And Mammon's only desire, in this age of the Temple of Take, is that people should consume.

As you can see, he has given Adam and Eve everything in the world they could possibly want.

But there's one thing they can't have, while they have everything they want. And that's responsibility and love for others.

If they had that and they didn't go along with Mammon, they'd already have shared out their incredible fortune to the rest of the starving, miserable world.

Now they want everything. Or so the serpent tells them; for, by introducing the concept of a responsibility to Eve, he ensures that she will lose it all.

– But that's not fair, we objected. I suppose we still felt sorry for Eve, with the monster, and Adam being stronger than her and almost beating her up when she used his poncy credit card.

– Why shouldn't Eve have a baby and a nice place to live? we demanded.

And Grandmother Dummer smiled.

– I'd forgotten that you're not ready to bear children yet, she said. But when you are, you'll see that the responsibility will lie fair and square with you. It will, in short, be all your fault.

I admit we didn't know what to make of this.

But, as Grandmother Dummer said, Eve went upstairs that evening – while Adam was still out staring at his parrot-fish and the piranha in the heated aquarium – and she opened the drawer of her dressing-table, converted from an escritoire belonging to Madame de Genlis, the first female pedagogue (also the first woman to own a writing-desk) – therefore a prime repository of female knowledge.

– Throw them away, Eve dear, said the Serpent's voice in her ear.

And she did.

She threw away all those little designer pills, which killed her ovulation and kept her pure and chaste each night for Adam to bite into, to consume along with all the exotic foods and drinks.

Eve's pills had been conceived for her by Salvador Dali and were in the shape of tiny apples dusted with silver and gold. Down the waste-disposal they went, leaving Eve happy and slightly out of breath at the rashness of her step.

But she had never looked more lovely than tonight. And when Frank brought Adam back from his silent moochings he held out his arms to Eve and begged her forgiveness for his sulk.

He apologized to Frank, too, and said he'd had a long day and he and Eve must go up to bed.

Like any best friend, Frank quite understood, even winking with Adam at the suggestion that he and Eve would fall instantly into a dreamless sleep.

And off to their rooms they all went.

– Did Adam *want* a baby? we said.

– Good God no, said Grandmother Dummer. The pack of brats he had with Lil are responsible for most of the damage taking place in the world today.

THE MARRIAGE OF
ADAM AND EVE

The easiest way to gauge a marriage is to start with the wedding photographs.

In this case, the video made by Bernardo Bertolucci, with music by Andrew Lloyd Webber and costumes by Emanuel.

How lovely the bride looks as she walks up the aisle, the swirl of cream satin exaggerating rather than concealing the twin boys that Eve will bear her lucky husband.

How radiant, under a diadem of Marie-Antoinette's diamonds.

And what a crowd of well-dressed, fashionable people! Adam must feel proud indeed.

He can send the video worldwide to business associates in Hong Kong, Hawaii and Hawick, and know he has shown himself off to his best advantage.

(As for the reception, need its splendours be recited? Federico Fellini has taken over for this second part and is clearly enjoying himself, dressing up the local policeman as the bride's mother and making Frank Blake dance the Dance of the Seven Veils in full make-up and jewellery.)

Babette's Feast is invoked several times when it comes to the wedding breakfast.

And the departure on honeymoon, in the biggest hot-air balloon in the world, shaped as a monstrous replica of the London Ritz hotel.

Oh how impressed those colleagues are going to be!

– And that, said Grandmother Dummer, is all there was to it.

Just a strip of celluloid and some dishy side-effects.

For the wedding didn't happen at all like that, you see. Adam spent his last penny on hiring the directors and actors; and as the last guest was filmed leaving gratefully from the fountain of Adam's wealth and generosity, the bailiffs were moving in from the other side. The street side, of course.

Because, you see, Lilith had taken Adam to the cleaners.

– Well, Elsie and I said, for we didn't really know what she meant, why was Adam made to lose his lovely house then? (And we didn't want to say so but we felt sorry for Eve in spite of all her silly tricks. After all, why shouldn't she have a baby, if she wants one? And why shouldn't she go on living in her beautiful house with Adam and the baby – or twin boys – if that's what it's got to be?)

– It just doesn't work out that way, Grandmother Dummer said. Lilith makes quite sure it doesn't, you know.

– I don't like Lilith, Elsie said.

– You may well turn into her, Grandmother Dummer said with a sad little laugh.

As Eve did, my dears.

The real wedding of Adam and Eve was in a grimy registrar's office, where the stale confetti from the wedding before hadn't even been cleared up and the registrar had such a bad head cold that he ended up marrying Adab and Ebe.

Eve is wearing – as you can see in the polaroid snap they had to beg the Indian cleaner to take with a camera borrowed from the Serpent and used for some of his more Satanic tricks, like blackmail – a faded denim boiler suit under which the twins kick, oblivious to the sudden change in their circumstances.

Adam is in a cheap blue suit hired from a secondhand shop in the big avenue near their home. This is in a building so near to falling down they have to use crampons and ropes to climb the rotting staircase.

When they get to the top they find a container – like a pig's trough, really – which the local aid centre fills with grub (too unspeakable to describe) for all the dwellers in the tenement.

Eve and Adam have obviously had their noses in this swill just before the wedding because there are stains on their clothes. They haven't brushed their hair for ages either, by the looks of it.

– How disgusting, Elsie and I said together. Why do they have to be like that?

– Poverty does funny things to people, Grandmother Dummer said. And they are terribly poor.

– But they're happy because they're in love, aren't they?

Grandmother Dummer says she's not sure about that. Their love had been to do with things and not with each other, that was the trouble, she said. So when the things were taken away, there was nothing left.

Except for the twins, of course.

So, while Eve stomps home on her own after the ceremony and Adam goes back to the dole queue, we'll follow Lilith on her travels; and we'll see just what Eve got herself into, by using the Gold Card that shouldn't really have been used at all. (Remember Mr Brown, the credit controller? He turned up the next day ready for his shared jacuzzi with Eve, only to find his lovely nymphet had donned a smock and a halo with Fabergé eggs set in the rim in pure gold. She told him, icily, to go away; but unfortunately, Adam was on his way back from the office with a ruby engagement ring first stolen from Aladdin's cave and buried with the secret of the Grand Duchess Anastasia, only to be dug up by President Gorbachev and presented to Adam as a measure of his gratitude for his new Soviet Satellite communications system. Adam saw Mr Brown and noted the number of his Volvo on his Cartier Must pad. After all, you never knew when evidence of this kind might come in handy.)

Lilith, as you also may remember, had gone to Venice.

It was heaven to sit in the Monaco Hotel, or just outside on the little terrace, with the gondolas bumping like friendly dogs against the wooden pier.

It was bliss to wander over the Bridge of Sighs while recalling that first, disastrous honeymoon with Adam.

And it was beyond belief wonderful to watch on the pocket computer as all Adam's holdings and shares and mines and property investments fell into Lilith's name.

For Lilith has the sharpest lawyer in the world, you see.

And he happens to spend one week a year in his private palazzo in Venice.

Lilith, realizing that Adam has installed Eve in a new mansion built to his own extremely lavish specification, decided to go and see her lawyer. There's no difficulty at all in persuading poor silly Eve to fix the ticket for her.

By doing that, Lilith has assured collusion. Nothing Adam can say or do will have any effect from now on.

In order to make an honest woman of Eve, now bearing his children, he has filed for divorce. But it is clear he is still supporting his first wife – even going so far as to use his own personal finance to do so: sending her on a trip to Italy is hardly a sign of estrangement, says her lawyer to Adam's lawyer via fax.

And that's just for starters.

For, you see, the divorce laws are back to front now. And whereas in the past the wicked behaviour of Lilith – or the adultery of Adam with Eve – would have been important factors in the contest, now everything is purely money.

The contestant with the best lawyer wins.

And Lilith's lawyer has conclusively proved that Lilith is not only due half of all Adam's wealth and possessions, but, as his true and lawful wife, is due the other half as well.

*

Which leaves Adam with nothing at all.

Things didn't come to this pretty pass as quickly as that, though. Money leaves an afterglow – a sort of lingering respect and reverence – and Adam and Eve, on expulsion from Eden, were invited to stay with friends all over the world.

They went to the sub-continent of India, where, on showing their faces as representatives of monotheism and the later Judaeo-Christian religions, they were threatened with a stoning and sent under armed guard to the border at night.

In the Boeing, sitting behind a row of fierce tribesmen who had boarded at Karachi with their own silver kettles for tea and their scimitars, Eve had to go behind the veil in order to disguise her identity.

Even so, she was recognized and there was nearly a sky riot over the Philippines.

For Eve is an acknowledged sinner by now. She has eaten of the fruit of the tree of the knowledge of good and evil; and even though her and Adam's definitions in this age of mass sexual experimentation may be different from the mullahs', they are a marked couple and will never find peace again.

Eve carries the seed of unrest in her. Abe and Cain, as they will surely be known, will do little to contribute to world peace.

The opposite, in fact.

And when you consider that Lilith is letting loose the full rage of her now-bulging portfolio on Adam and Eve, the future looks bleak indeed.

In the meantime, though, they spend a fortnight in Brunei with the richest man in the world (the Sultan makes Adam an honorary citizen; but unfortunately, when the irredeemability of his poverty becomes known, this is turned into an edict to throw Adam in prison if he should present himself at the border in the innocent hope of going on another tiger hunt).

They spend all of three weeks in the Caribbean, wining and dining with royalty in Mustique. They accept the hospitality of the Marxists of Grenada, who are under the mistaken impression that Adam controls the resources of the USA. And they stay on the sinister island of Bequia, where the local witch doctor tries to charm Adam's fortune back into existence. (Unsuccessful: Adam is left with a bill for a new-born baby and a packet of Price's wax candles imported from Barbados.)

And they stay with a French marquess, who gives them the run of his château for as long as they want it.

Here, among the vineyards and olives, you might think that Adam and Eve could relax indefinitely.

But they are doomed to wander, exiled from the love and protection of their god.

The château catches fire one night – Lilith's doing, this: she has made a hurricane tour of the Middle East and caught up with the adulterers at last in Bordeaux – and they are evacuated, dripping wet from the pumps and scorched by the flames that Lil, disguised as Mrs Rochester, has wrapped around the hangings of their four-poster.

Never forget the fury of a first wife abandoned.

*

So, by the time the erring couple arrive in London, enough time has passed for the news of Adam's poverty to sink in thoroughly.

He arrives home – that is, at the house of a rich necrophiliac friend who is prepared briefly to put Adam and Eve up, in the hope that they will find bodies for his wilder lusts if they are desperate enough for food and accommodation (and who would know better where to find a fresh corpse than the mother-to-be of the first murderer?) – Adam arrives home, as I say, to find a letter dismissing him from the last directorship still in his name.

Lilith has taken over the company, which sells dispensers – of coffee, coke and the like – with her new-found wealth.

She also spread the rumour that Adam had plans to dispense unpasteurised milk and non-fluoridated water from the dispensers, thus causing damage to the population as a whole.

With SatelHaven, Lilith's task was even easier: disguised as a meteor, Lil encircled Adam's satellites and garbled their messages, so that President Bush received a sudden video of Raisa Gorbachev on the lavatory and the Ayatollah of Iran was given the full Christmas carol service from Westminster Abbey.

Subscriptions were cancelled by the million. Sateldishes, designed by Paloma Picasso, were hurled to the ground by dissatisfied customers.

And all this between joining the Ugandan magic women's army, to fortify her strength between spells of vindictiveness and devilish cunning.

She joined the Nuer, too, in that part of West Africa where

crocodiles lie in wait for exiles' ankles in the dozy palaces of the Ivory Coast; and she marched, accoutred as a man, at the head of the tribal troops, several thousand of whom she had bought on the afternoon of her arrival.

Do you really think Adam and Eve had a chance against a force like Lil's?

No, nor do I, said Grandmother Dummer when we had shaken our heads in wonderment. It is left to them only to go from miserable bed-and-breakfast accommodation to wrecked council flat, squatted by drug dealers and skin-heads, to – and they're lucky to find this – a semi-derelict housing association building on a plot of land where sub-sidence threatens the lives of the inhabitants regularly.

They're grateful for the organization which comes to fill their feed bucket every other day.

And by the time the divorce finally comes through and they can marry (Lil has, of course, held up the proceedings as long as she possibly could), Eve is grateful, too, for the pile of yellowing, second-hand nappies a well-wisher leaves outside her door. The birth of the twins is very imminent indeed.

– I don't see how you can say we'd ever be like Lilith, Elsie said when we'd thought about the sad fate of Adam and Eve. Surely – we couldn't be.

Oh, I'll show you how, Grandmother Dummer said, before suggesting a walk to the little church and back through the woods before tea.

LILITH

To begin with, Grandmother Dummer said, as we stood in the church (Elsie and I wishing we could go to Truro, to that tea-room where they have gorgeous shop-made chocolate cake, and not the home-made scones and jams everyone goes on about) – to begin with, of course, Eve did everything she could to save her marriage.

She'd read all the women's magazines and in spite of all the very real difficulties she was up against, like poverty, she was determined to make the best of life with a family.

The armchair, salvaged from the dump in the street where they were pulling down sheltered housing for the elderly and infirm and building luxury flats with ateliers for interior decorators, had only three legs, so Eve, in a moment of cheerful inspiration, as recommended by the women's magazines, sawed them all off and covered the seat with a cloth the fishmonger had thrown out after using it for swabbing down his counter. A floor-chair! was how she described her creation, when other young mums called round with their kids and puffed and panted up the stairs.

– And a floor table, Eve went on with a delighted laugh as the strip of sagging formica, found in the flat when they arrived, finally gave way under the strain of a meagre plate of sandwiches.

– What fun! Eve said. Let's pretend we're in a Japanese restaurant!

Eve tried, too, to keep a cheerful and exciting sex life going with Adam. After all, they had loved so much and so deliciously in Eden. On one occasion, as Eve fondly remembers, Adam had covered her body entirely with rose petals – crystallized in sugar and dipped in violet water, naturally – and licked them all off her.

– Goodness, Elsie and I said. (We were still thinking of that cream tea and synthetic cake, I suppose.)

Another time they'd literally swung from the chandelier.

Of course, Eve was light as a feather then. And now – well, what with the twins and the diet of pretty solid carbohydrate, she's heavy.

Very heavy. Adam refers to her as a whale.

And because he has lost all his money and he is miserable and he lives with a fat woman who can't stop crying when she's not pretending to be cheerful, Adam decides that everything that's happened to him is Eve's fault.

– You see, said Grandmother Dummer as we looked up at her in the little church, and about to protest again at the unfairness of it all, we're this very minute standing in a building which is consecrated to the belief that it was all Eve's fault.

Whereas this poor mermaid – and she went over to stroke the head of that laughing nymph with guiltless, pagan eyes – whereas this lass was taken over by the Christian Church when they had no right to lay hands on her at all.

Before the Church elders pronounced on the wickedness of Eve, this goddess of the sea and the stream, this nereid, was worshipped as the sole progenitor and giver of life.

People believed that pregnancy came through the wind, or water as it bubbled up in a spring.

They worshipped the Mother Goddess and Earth was the mother of them all. If it hadn't been for the Serpent telling Eve that the man in the Garden of Eden could father children, the natural balance of things would have gone on forever.

But you can't blame Eve for listening to the Serpent.

Once she did, though, she gradually came to lose more and more power, until she ended up trying to please a cross unemployed man in a crumbling slum, with screaming brats and not enough to eat.

So – were Abe and Cain terribly naughty? we wanted to know. (We'd secretly decided never to let us ourselves become like Eve. I knew Elsie wanted to be an airline pilot. And – because I loved the sea – I was going to be a deep-sea diver and go down so deep I'd find the source of those mysterious pinkish lights that glow – so it's said – on the ocean floor.)

This mutual if unspoken decision must have cheered us up, because Grandmother Dummer burst out laughing.

– I wish luck to both of you, she said, without bothering to answer the question. Biology is not destiny. No. But you'll find that all the old categories – stereotypes – are still there for women and every single one of them is a pitfall.

And one of the most dangerous moments is when a woman, either intentionally or in spite of herself, changes over from one category to another.

This is what was happening to Eve.

When she'd made love with Adam in Eden they had, as I say, tried every position in the book – the Kama Sutra, if you like, or Shere Hite's latest offering.

One thing they'd never done, though.

Eve lying on top.

It had always been the missionary position (if not some of the exotic variants) and now Eve felt she was the wiser and stronger of the two – after all, she'd given birth to twins and she had to mend their clothes and try to cook on a shared stove in the fungus-ridden hallway of the tenement – so it was time she was the missionary and Adam the ignorant heathen.

The more Adam resisted, the harder Eve tried.

She woke in the middle of the night and found herself half-astride Adam, who even in his sleep fought her off with all his might.

Adam might be weak now, you see, but even if he lived in a cardboard crate he'd make sure he was still in the dominating position with Eve. It was only natural, after all.

Natural since the Fall, that is.

Now, said Grandmother Dummer, you must be wondering what happened to Frank Blake. The friendly neighbourhood snake.

Well, he's been round of course, bearing gifts of impossible luxury like a packet of sliced ham; and he soon sees what the matter is.

Eve is ground down, as he sees it, and Adam wants to grind her down further. Eve, on the other hand, while thinking her sexual innovations will bring renewed excitement to the marriage, actually wants to show her contempt for Adam's impotence in the market-place by placing herself as a chairman rather than a broad. She wants to sit on Adam, as the snake sees. She wants to rule the rooster.

Frank Blake takes Eve aside. He hisses in her ear. Meanwhile, Cain throws Abe down the stairs in the first of his many assassination attempts and Adam stumps down in a rage to pick him up. (This is woman's work. My, how claustrophobic it can get when both partners are home!)

– You need a holiday on your own, the Serpent says.

– I mean, Eve, quite frankly, look at you.

Here Frank Blake has certainly scored a goal. For it's not only that Eve is vast, with arms that look as if they've been blown up for a party and are in the process of sagging down again. It's that, more and more lately, Eve has been seeing the monster's face in the mirror when she goes to the bathroom to brush her teeth (well, what else is there to do when there's only a basin and a cracked glass: the WC is three floors down and it's years since the last bath was taken out and sold as an 'original feature' to a rock group who suddenly made good after thirty years in the wilderness?)

Brushing her teeth, Eve sees nearly every time now the mad, enraged and bitter eyes of the monster. Like abandoned quarries filled with acid rain and deposits of radioactive slime, those eyes look back at her from a moon-scape of pitted cheeks and a nose like a hang-glider who's got snagged in a tree.

Frank Blake sees Lilith.

And he says he'll bring a brochure next time he comes, and lend Eve the money to go away.

Have we heard all this before? The last thing unhappy wives need are holidays, I can tell you.

They need money, jobs and self-respect.

But Eve is such a silly that when the Serpent says she'll be going to a spa where she'll be pounded and treated with herbal body washes and got back into trim generally, she accepts his kind offer with alacrity.

Isn't it funny that she'll do anything to keep Adam, like the magazines say she should.

Why?

It's not even as if he's nice to her. When she blows her nose he mutters 'Christ!' instead of asking if she might be getting a cold.

When she laughs at something (pretty rare these days) he glowers at her so hard she thinks she's committed a crime.

And when the twins make a racket – as they do for approximately twenty hours out of twenty-four – Eve knows very definitely that it's her fault.

This is how she knows so definitely.

The noise of the fighting and screaming twins has led Adam more and more out of the house.

Now, if you want to keep your man, as the magazines say, to see him leaving the house is hardly an encouraging start.

But what is Eve to do? There is no money for a child-minder. Local groups are full up (and there's a chance that Cain's reputation, spreading fast, would keep them full anyway).

Eve is stuck. And her heart bleeds for poor Adam, as he tramps the rainy streets and queues for a soup at the stall run by the Salvation Army. Where did their love go? How to get it back?

Eve consults fortune tellers, one of whom is so sorry for Eve she gives her services for free.

And, as she stares into the crystal ball, she sits bolt upright suddenly and adjusts her pince-nez.

For, pictured in the concave glass, and walking along as if he hadn't a care in the world, is Adam.

The worst of it is that he has his arm round the slender waist of a blonde.

Eve stares. She recognizes the blonde – the daughter of a Cabinet Minister, who had come to Adam and Eve's parties at Eden and who is called Brigid.

Frigid Brigid. Eve remembers the joke as she fights back her tears.

Not so frigid after all, then?

Eh? How dare you? Eve shouts at Adam when he comes home two days later, smelling of Poison and with a lipstick smudge on his shirt that looks like a designer label spelling BRIGID.

– How could you? Eve gasps. The children. How can you do this to them?

But Adam just shrugs in the face of Eve's rage and the bawling twins, who have been locked in the flat since Eve started to cry and couldn't cope with taking them out to the muggers' playground any longer.

And he sees Lilith, a hideous, accusing monster. Adam hates and fears the monster.

So he goes.

Three days later, children, Frank Blake arrives with the holiday brochure and Eve grabs it greedily.

But it's too late. Eve has lost Adam and that's it.

Even the kindest neighbours and shopkeepers treat Eve differently now that Adam has gone.

She couldn't keep her man. One way or another, it must be her fault.

HARLOT

I don't know whether Grandmother Dummer waited until we were all in the Lawks-A-Mercy-Me Tea Rooms in Truro before telling us the next stage in the story of Eve for the simple reason that we would understand temptation better in those surroundings – or whether she wanted to take us away from the place where she lived and where the little church on the hill exercised such a strong pull on anyone who came near it.

Whichever it was, we were soon too tied up in the business of deciding between macaroons the size of satellites and éclairs that were bursting with secret creams and custards to feel very shocked at Eve's decision in life.

In the early stages of the tea – while Grandmother Dummer was eating her scones and we were allowed the amazing indulgence of actually starting the meal with the shop-made cake, studded with artificial choc chips, such as we had been dreaming about all week – we did ask if Eve couldn't have gone out and got herself a job when Adam left.

After all, every time you turn on the TV there's a programme about getting women back to work.

– Oh yes, said Grandmother Dummer. Eve tried to work, all right. But you see, whatever they may say, to be a single mother of twins who are going through a difficult phase – and I'm afraid all Abe and Cain's life was a difficult phase – doesn't get you a job very easily.

Eve started with temping. But just as she sat to take dictation in a job and the boss explained the work she would be expected to do over the coming week, the desk phone would bleep and there would be an emergency paging for Eve.

One or other of the twins – and they had, of course, developed a private language which their mother was as far from understanding as anyone else – would have broken a collarbone by falling down the stairs; or have bumps the size of a robin's egg all over his chest so the crèche wanted him out on grounds of contagion; or an innocent passer-by, lamed by one of Cain's charges with his sub-machine-gun, had had their lawyer call to announce legal proceedings against the custodian of Cain, who was, as you don't need reminding, Eve.

The number of times Eve swore she would get her own back on Adam, come what may. Leaving the twins muttering and signalling in their weird code, she goes out on her fiftieth jobless day to the post office to collect the dwindling family allowance, and to stalk the streets in the upmarket areas of town for her husband and his paramour.

What is Adam doing? you ask.

Adam has become a politician. Living with the Cabinet Minister's daughter, his pious announcements that he is waiting only for his divorce from Eve for the happy day to be settled for himself and Brigid appear regularly in the press.

Maddeningly, Eve can't find where Adam and Brigid actually do live. (Adam has been cunning, and has concealed himself just where you'd least think of looking for him: in the very poorest area of the city, where an armed guard is on twenty-four-hour duty. Brigid finds the whole thing pretty sexy, and can boast to friends that she lives in the last place on earth that can ever be gentrified.)

But on this day, Eve does find where Adam lives.

She has been sent by the Social Security Department, who have regretfully informed Eve that the building in which she has been resident since the birth of the twins has been condemned and will be pulled down to make way for an Inland Marina and Pizza Piazza project, designed by an architect by appointment to the Prince of Wales to resemble the gingerbread cottages inhabited by plantation slaves in the West Indies at the end of the eighteenth century.

Eve must go. And this blackspot of an area, infamous den of 'crack' dealers and used-needle AIDS sufferers, will be her new home.

It's the end of the line for Eve. She walks very slowly, pushing the enormous weight of the twins before her in a double pushchair, like a monstrous never-ending pregnancy.

On the way to this plague pit of an area, Eve sees all the other abandoned children – for she knows very well, like so many of the parents in fairy tales who, when they can no longer support them, take their children out to the forest and leave them there to die, that she will do this to Cain and little Abie too – on the way to this desolate world's end, where scratched and sprayed on fissured walls are the words 'Abandon Hope All Ye who Enter Here', Eve suddenly sees Adam crossing the road.

– More tea? says the waitress in the Lawks-A-Mercy-Me Tea Rooms. But Elsie and I are drinking chocolate cappucino, with frothy white foam at the top, and we shake our heads and say no. Grandmother Dummer, on the other hand, says she'll have a double Scotch on the Rocks and be quick about it.

– We don't serve alcohol, says the waitress, shocked, and Grandmother Dummer laughs and says it was only a joke, because it's just what Adam said when he, too, had seen Eve and his own two sons and had darted back across the road into his house, where the butler paid for by Brigid's father had asked Mr First if he could get anything for him? He looked as if he'd seen a ghost!

– And he had, in a way, Grandmother Dummer said. The only trouble being that Eve is still alive, however many times he wishes otherwise.

– He can't want the twins dead too, Elsie and I say. We're worried already that these poor children will be left to fend for themselves – as all children would be worried. And the amount of chocolate we've drunk and eaten is beginning to make us feel sick.

– Which one is the eldest? we say when Grandmother Dummer, very frighteningly, won't tell us that Adam loves his children really and wants only to care for them for ever.

– It's a question of opinion as to which came first, says Grandmother Dummer.

Cain, who is Evil.

Cain, who is the man who stays in one place and builds up the fortunes with which to starve and bully the weak. Cain, the first capitalist.

Or Abel, the wandering man, who is Good. Who has no possessions and does not accumulate wealth, and takes only what he needs from the kingdom of animals and vegetables.

Cain, the murderer. Abel the victim. Which is the first son of Adam First?

But no one can remember. Because the midwife was late – and drunk – and Adam was out canoodling with Brigid just at the moment of their birth.

So sometimes Eve says Cain is the elder and the ruler of the world.

And sometimes, on the days of relative peace and a modicum of sunshine, she says it's Abe after all.

– So you can hardly blame Eve for succumbing to temptation. After all, she has already been blamed for bringing down the house of Adam, and she is suffering all the horror of finding herself Lilith after all.

– But who exactly was Lilith? we asked Grandmother Dummer. And what exactly did Eve succumb to? we wondered, when she seems to have become the sort of person few would wish to tempt.

– Ha. You'll see, said Grandmother Dummer.

And she explained to us that Lilith had been the first wife

God had made for Adam, and she had turned out to be a terrible mistake.

She answered back.

She took all Adam's favourite compact discs and threw them off the side of a cliff when they were holidaying in the South of France one year.

And when they lay down at night, Adam would wake as if in a nightmare and see Lilith sitting astride him as if he were no more than a broomstick, a sort of temporary transport to a witches' bacchanalia. To be discarded as soon as she reached her wild ecstasy.

It wouldn't do at all, and God even apologized to Adam for what he had put him through.

He sent Lilith off into the wilderness. She became Hecate, Queen of the Night. All the wretched orphaned unwanted starving children in the world belong to Lilith, who is in turn a vile mother with sour milk in her breasts and a box of poison viruses to release into the world if her children grow too many.

She is jealous, too. Surely, if God meant her as Adam's mate, that's what she should be. And he only made her as strong as Adam in order to find a perfect balance between a man and a woman, didn't he?

But God saw that equality wasn't what he – or Adam – could cope with at all.

To make Eve, he simply asked Adam to go to sleep so that he could remove a rib.

And when Adam woke up, there was a smiling, submissive part of him just waiting to do as it was told.

No wonder Adam didn't like it when Eve tried to get on

top of him. Husbands don't like their second wives reminding them of the first, that's plain.

And of course the joke is that when Adam sees Eve in the street outside his house, he does actually think it's Lilith, so ghastly has she become.

And the twins are no more than members of that army of vagrants that every big city has grown used to now: in Cain and Abe he sees the thieves and petty muggers of the rough streets where he lives.

Eve goes home and howls with rage and frustration.

Her rage has become the rage of eternal exile, her sadness is the sadness of Satan's handmaid, abandoned to evil, removed for all time from love and the power of good.

Her revenge and triumph are those of Judith as she holds up the head of Holofernes, and of Salome as she drinks the blood from the severed neck of John the Baptist.

Her milk will sustain the tribe of wanderers condemned in perpetuity to roam the world and to find no home – for isn't she Hagar, surrogate wife of Abraham, who was cast out in the desert with her son Ishmael when her services were no longer required?

– What have I done to deserve this? roars Eve, as she staggers to the fridge and takes out an entire platter of profiteroles stolen from the pâtisserie where she is some-times lucky enough to obtain work as a part-time waitress, ladling *mille-feuilles* and rhum babas on to the plates of those richer and more privileged than she.

– My God, my God, get me out of this! bellows Eve, as she downs a gallon of duty-free whisky lifted from the airport where she is sometimes lucky enough to get part-time work cleaning the international scum from the table tops and vacuuming the farts out of the airport seating complex before another wave of Club Classers turn up for mineral water and Café Hag.

No, Eve hasn't realized that her powers have grown with the identity of Lilith. Her slightest sob brings down a whole row of artisans' houses just renovated south of the park for the new work-at-home brigade. Her gusts of venom blow right into the Houses of Parliament and members' toupées blow off on to the floor.

Heads of State all over the world wake with acute anxiety attacks when Lilith/Eve screams in her desire for vengeance – on Adam and the world.

And her god, the god who works night and day against the true God, comes strolling up the steep stairs to Eve's condemned flat and knocks on the frail door. He is holding a couple of really dishy dresses, one in chiffon with a low back and the other in scarlet raw silk, with a very short mini-skirt indeed.

– My dear Eve, says Frank Blake as he hands over black suspender belt, high heels and a make-up case that would have kept all the Bluebell girls happy for a year; how nice to hear you call on me again.

Eve takes these garments and looks at them doubtfully, like an elephant being told to climb into a pair of teenager's panties.

As she stands there, Cain, who has smelt trouble, runs up and bites Frank Blake on the shin. But he's disconcerted to find that no yell of pain follows his action and that the taste of snakeskin is very nasty indeed. Being a coward, as we know all bullies really are, Cain then bursts into tears.

Abe, meanwhile, is looking carefully at this new character in his life. He has second sight, like many rootless, wandering gypsy races, and he senses that Frank Blake will be very important to his future, one way or another.

– I'll take the boys off your hands, Frank Blake says smoothly. And this is for you, too. He takes from a briefcase a tall can and a plastic spoon.

– Here, my dear, is the Cambridge diet. Come on, boys, or we'll be late.

– But where is he taking them? Elsie and I said. We were quite worried by now; and as we'd already succumbed to temptation in the Tea Rooms and eaten over a kilo of chocolate each, we thought that whatever it was that Eve was being told to do, she certainly oughtn't to do it. (The kind of thought that comes after over-indulgence and not before; and true, alas, as we were to discover, of the new profession which the Serpent was urging Eve to take up.)

– The oldest profession, Grandmother Dummer said gently, afraid of shocking us after all.

And Frank Blake simply told Eve he was taking the boys to live with their father for a while.

After all, Adam is their father, isn't he?

Or isn't he? No one knows what happened in the jacuzzi that afternoon in Eden, do they, children?

No man can ever be one hundred per cent sure of the paternity of his child. That's why men have locked women up, over the centuries; and in Muslim countries they tie them into portable homes as well, all curtain and conceal-ing blanket in case of temptation.

Adam is the head of the family, whatever else, and regis-tered as the father of the twins. He has paid no maintenance whatever since running off with Brigid.

No doubt Brigid wouldn't like it if he used some of the money she hands out airily to her darling while he gets back on his feet – and he will! he will! – on doing something so mundane as helping to support his wife and children.

And the boys need a father, after all.

So Eve gives in and says she wants access at the weekend, at least.

– But of course, murmurs the Serpent, as he holds out gleaming toy robots to the boys, to tempt them down the stairs. I will make certain that you have all the time with them that you wish.

And they go. Now, said Grandmother Dummer, standing up and getting ready to leave the Tea Rooms and make for the bus stop for the long ride home: now for the temptation.

Eve's flat was condemned, remember. She had twenty-one days in which to find other accommodation. And she had three notes in her bag: notes of the lowest denomi-nation. After the landlord had been, hot on the heels of the Serpent, Eve had no money left at all.

She wouldn't want to sell those lovely dresses, would she?

– No, we both said, although we knew somehow this was wrong.

The Cambridge diet took exactly twenty-one days to slim Eve down.

Imagine how happy she was when she could slip into those infinitely lovely garments and go out into the world as a pretty woman instead of a monster.

– Did she look like Eve again? we asked anxiously. (Somehow we thought if she could go back to being Eve then all the bad things that had happened could miraculously disappear and she could return to her beautiful home again.)

– Not really, Grandmother Dummer said, after a pause for reflection as we walked along the rainy street and stood under the bus shelter.

Eve had been given all that facial equipment, you see. Well, obviously she just had to have one try at it, just for fun. You would, wouldn't you?

– Yes, we said. No doubt we were convinced this time.

So Eve had the peachiest skin and the longest eyelashes and the brightest blue eye shadow and the sweetest pink blusher and the most ruby red lips …

But where was she to go?

– You can hardly blame her, Grandmother Dummer said. For stopping at the corner and admiring her reflection in the supermarket window. There's no full-length mirror in the flat, of course. And the little strip of jagged glass above the cracked basin has just been thrown out, along with all the rest of Eve's pathetic furniture, for the twenty-one days to the end of the lease are up.

When a car stops. Fancy that! It's Mr Brown. Remember him, girls? Mr Brown of Credit Control. He is driving a Porsche the colour of the under-belly of a shark. And he stops when he sees Eve.

I mean, who wouldn't?

– And she gets into the car? we said. Why is that so tempting, Grandmother Dummer? For we didn't much like the idea of Mr Brown.

– Exactly, said Grandmother Dummer. But what else could Eve do?

We thought about this for a while and came reluctantly to the conclusion there wasn't much alternative. To cheer ourselves up, we reminded Grandmother Dummer that Eve would be able to see the twins at the weekend.

– I'm afraid not, said Grandmother Dummer. You see, the Serpent just took them to the area where Adam lives and dumped them in the street.

We were silent for quite a long time after Grandmother Dummer had stopped speaking. And I suppose, in a way, we wanted her to be silent now, too. Children can take just so much news from the other world, the world beyond puberty where nothing is as it seems and everything could go the other way: the world of the terrifyingly unpredictable grown-ups.

So for several days we played on the beach and built sandcastles and waded out when the tide was low over rock pools where shrimps lay as transparent as the sky and anemones waved their stubby red and purple fingers.

It was all such a long way from the life-story of Eve, the story Grandmother Dummer had begun because we insisted – and there was no going back now.

And one evening, later in that mild and beautiful Cornish summer, she did. We ran in from the beach and sat by her on

the low sill of her sitting-room that looks out to sea –
because something told us that the story was about to
continue and we knew we had to be there.

– It didn't take Eve long to realize that Mr Brown was one
of the most evil men in the world, said Grandmother
Dummer. You remember she got into his car right outside
the supermarket at the end of her street?

Yes, we said. We remembered. But over the past days we'd
been so busy trying not to think of the dreadful fate of Abe
and Cain that we'd deliberately not thought of Eve. Grandmother Dummer said we must.

– Don't forget, children, that Eve will do all she can to
get the twins back. In the meantime, she must find the
money. The only trouble is that Mr Brown takes nearly
all her money, as soon as she earns it.

We were aghast at this, of course. How *can* someone take
your earnings? What *right* have they? And for a moment we
wanted to rise up and run off in search of the wicked Mr
Brown and give him such a punishment that he'd never do it
again.

– That's Lilith speaking, said Grandmother Dummer
with a loud laugh. Yes, I often feel that revenge is the only
way. But you see, in Eve's case, she is literally powerless.

For a while, that is.

◆

Mr Brown has installed Eve in a flat.

It's a flat right in the centre of the capital, where embass-
ies and big business and haute couture all meet. It costs as

much for a dinner for two in one of the many discreetly lit restaurants and clubs as it does to support an entire family for a year in the wretched neighbourhood from which Eve has just come. Even the *grissini* – those are the Italian bread sticks the film directors and multi-corporation men like to munch on while they're waiting for their exquisitely presented plates – are baked in the Po Valley and flown in by private supersonic jet, so they're still warm by the time the first PA makes the first booking.

Eve's flat is in a block overlooking these distinguished establishments.

So it's only a step or two, you see, from the *petits fours* – which come after the coffee, my dears, and are sweets and tiny cakes with a crystallized cherry on top – to the cherry in the apartment building above.

– What do you mean? we said. But Grandmother Dummer just said she'd used a rather naughty word for Eve's private parts and we should forget all about cherries straight away.

– Did the men want to eat Eve then? we said. And we couldn't help seeing a lovely pink body, made entirely from sugar like the pink mice Santa Claus put in our stockings every Christmas; and fat balding men eating their way right up the legs to poor Eve's heart.

– Yes, in a way. They're paying to have her, said Grandmother Dummer. So there isn't much in it.

And when they've gone, Mr Brown comes in and beats Eve up if she doesn't hand over all the money. (Don't forget, Mr Brown isn't a credit controller for nothing. He understands that each minute money goes uninvested means lack of interest. And Mr Brown is very interested indeed in taking Eve's earnings before she's had time to have any idea of escape.)

Mr Brown owns several women in this way, says Grandmother Dummer, as we swear that we will never in any circumstances find ourselves in Eve's.

So of course he's quite rich by now.

All the same, he always wants more. So he makes Eve dress as an Indian elephant boy and sit on her customers in a howdah; and for that he charges double.

Then, some businessmen like to be badly treated, you know. It's something to do with feeling guilty about making all that money, I expect. And Mr Brown starts a weekend course, as he calls it, where the businessmen are locked in coffins with a hole at each end and Eve has to tempt them with flashes of her naked bum and the like. While another tart – for that, I fear, children, is what Eve has become – shouts abuse and whips them if they try to climb out.

– How terrible, we said. (I think it was at that moment that Elsie and I decided not to grow up, ever.)

Not everyone is like that, Grandmother Dummer was at pains to tell us – because she must have guessed our feelings. There *is* good in the world. And, as it comes to everyone, so it came to Eve.

In the shape of the tart on the floor above, Sally by name. (Mr Brown didn't know, when he nicknamed her Salome, that she would strip him of his assets with greater speed than even the most cursory dance of the Seven Veils. For all the months he had enjoyed standing over poor Sally as she writhed and belly-danced, and the businessmen crooned and jeered and threw money into a brass Arabian pot for the sharing of her favours, he would get his come-uppance in the end; and all these men coming up Sally night and day had turned her pretty cunning.)

Of course she has a heart of gold. Many tarts have; mainly, I suppose, because they give away a great deal more than they get.

But on top of that, Sally has enterprise. (Even if, as we shall see, her plans were sometimes a little too ambitious.)

The day she knocks on Eve's door has been one of the most exhausting yet. Eve has had to entertain a convention of fundamentalist Evangelical preachers from the Middle West; and an entire division of Arsenal United.

Tonight, after a brief respite for toilet and grooming – yes, Mr Brown has installed a jacuzzi in the flat: how he loves to look through the one-way video system at his captive money-spinner – Eve has a delegation from Mount Athos and must fuck, one by one, those ecclesiastical beards.

For her pains, the priests will dole out a heavy chastisement. (But even this is preferable to the fate of the wretched Yvonne from two storeys above, who found herself the unfortunate recipient of the passionate love of a ninety-six-year-old Pappas, who cut off her breasts and smuggled her in a *kelim* into the all-male Greek monastic reserve.)

So Eve, as I say, is tired and her heart is heavy. How will she ever regain her children or live again in the outside world? How will she make even the smallest amount of money?

When Mr Brown takes her out shopping, new dresses and

fine lingerie are all charged to his account. Even the simplest domestic items go on his Tristar Super Platinum card.

And the phone is connected via satellite to Mr Brown wherever he goes, so if Eve tries to ring out and fix an escape he can hear her and press the wipe button, which replaces Eve's voice with the angelic sound of Kiri Te Kanawa singing the Ave Maria.

Oh how Eve wishes she had a) never met Adam and got into this jam, and b) stayed in her job, working hard to become a businesswoman in due course.

Well, it's too late for that anyway.

Eve needs a break, or she may break herself. And when the bell rings as she's still in the jacuzzi – where she's fallen asleep from sheer exhaustion – she honestly feels she'd rather jump from the window of the apartment on to the parked Rollses and Bentleys hundreds of feet below than go on leading this life one minute longer.

The bell goes again, though, and in her bathrobe, face shiny and eyes bleary with fatigue, Eve staggers to the door. (She knows, alas, that the Greek Fathers won't be put off by her appearance, however unorthodox it may be.) And, turning the lock seven times in the security combination, she opens up.

There, resplendent in the red wig she is made to wear for her impersonation of Irma La Douce for relatives of minor royalty and old-age pensioners from Torquay, stands Sally.

Sally is carrying a laundry basket. Nothing unusual in that: Mr Brown likes his worker bees, as he laughingly calls poor Eve and the others, to occupy themselves with changing sheets, vacuuming, and cleaning out the giant Agas in the basement of the block of flats where the men who like to regress to childhood in their sexual fantasies and have roly-poly pudding and spotted dick either fed to them or thrown at them, get their suet steamed.

Oh the long hours Eve and Sally have worked together in these menial tasks before going wearily upstairs and changing into negligée or harem gown for their men!

– Yes, said Grandmother Dummer when Elsie opened her mouth to speak, I know that sounds just like a housewife's life. And quite honestly, there isn't all that much in it. Scrubbers are just as useful for cleaning out kitchen sinks.

Anyway, Eve isn't surprised to see the laundry basket. But, fond of Sally though she is, she just hasn't the energy to go down to the massive laundry room, fitted out as a Victorian place of torture, with the original coppers and the great bowls with blue rinse to get the sheets whiter than white which Mr Brown has installed down there in preference to modern machines for the sake of elder statesmen who remember their first deflowering in the laundry room of an ancestral home at the turn of the century.

No, Eve just hasn't the strength to pound and scrub, with all these bearded patriarchs shortly to come down on her. So she smiles weakly and says sorry, but she can't.

– Oh don't be silly, Eve, Sally says. Just help me with these. And then it's Room Nineteen.

Now, this frightens Eve very much indeed. The notorious Room Nineteen, on the very top storey of the apartment block, is somewhere she has always refused to go – and it's the one room where Mr Brown, for love or money or any amount of bribes or harassment, can't get his other 'employees' to go to, either.

There have been too many rumours, for one thing.

Some say that the necrophiliac Count von Cruel keeps Room Nineteen for his own purposes (he's the 'friend', remember, with whom Adam and Eve stayed briefly in the course of their fall from Eden).

If this is so, then Eve would literally rather be seen dead by anyone other than him. Even if, since they last met, the Cruel Count has left more than one wife in a coma – and has inherited, from these brain-dead millionairesses, enough money to spring Eve from this squalid place with just a thousandth of his daily spending money.

But Eve is too spooked to go to Room Nineteen and that's all there is to it. She doesn't want to lie in a coffin while the Count screws down the lid and then rises up from under the bier and screws her.

– I should think not, we said. (At this point I honestly think that Elsie had abandoned deep-sea diving or airline piloting as a future career and was considering becoming an anchorite. As for me, I vowed to become a vet and dedicate myself to animals, the first love of children, and no wonder.)

– Yes, says Sally. It's worth it tonight, Eve. I'll explain when we get up there.

And she hands Eve a waiter's outfit from the laundry basket – black tuxedo, white tie and all; while, for herself, she winds a sheet round herself and takes the make-up off her face, and there she is, as convincing a corpse as you're likely to find. Red hair and all – she laughs when she sees Eve's expression and says she always did fancy herself as Lady Lazarus.

– Now, children, Grandmother Dummer says, you may say that Eve and Sally played a naughty trick on Count von Cruel – but honestly, what else could they do?

They couldn't know, could they, that the tables were about to be turned on the Count. (Or maybe Sally did, but no matter.) That the Grim Reaper, tired of lingering about the beds in luxury clinics that were occupied by the Count's ex-wives, was going to come and claim the Don Juan of the life-support machine all for himself.

And they couldn't know that a young lawyer (a pin-stripe suit always sat well on Sally) who was also the Count's very personal notary, would be in Room Nineteen, either.

But he was.

And, just as Sally opened the door of Room Nineteen with infinite care (she and Eve had gone up in the service lift, Sally disguised as a male servant with a laundry basket of heavy linen), the Count, who was lying in his funereal bed, draped as always in black crêpe and festooned with small wreaths of yew and other evergreens, gave a loud groan and died.

– Quick, says our Salome, our bright Sally, who has her red wig off in a trice and over the eyes of the young notary. And – quick, quick! – Sally has that young man stripped and trussed up like a chicken and packed into the laundry basket, which – yes, you guessed – Eve is told to trundle as nonchalantly as possible to the service lift.

Which, after what seems an age, comes bearing a party of Japanese tourists in search of the Tower of London room, where Mr Brown has laid on for their benefit and at enormous expense to them a parade of all the wives of Henry the Eighth.

For all Eve's fear of bumping into Mr Brown, there's only a young notary in Room Nineteen when she gets back there – apart from the defunct Count von Cruel, of course.

– I need a witness for this last will and testament, says the figure in the notary's clothing, and looks round masterfully at Eve.

– Ah, Jack, you'll do, Sally goes on rapidly, shaking her head at ceiling and walls all with bugging devices planted by Mr Brown.

– A witness, Jack, says Sally in her deep voice. Sign here.

– Need I tell you, girls, said Grandmother Dummer, with a slight smile, that the infamous Count von Cruel had left his entire fortune to Sally and Eve?

And need I tell you that it took all of four minutes for Mr Brown's detectives, trained in the SS and the SAS and the dungeons of Turkey, to get the truth out of the forgers? (But it was a good try, anyway.)

And precisely four seconds for Mr Brown's bouncer, ex-trainer of Mike Tyson, to throw the impostors out into the street, wearing all they had come in with – that is to say, a thin dress and no coat at all.

And it's snowing.

*

– Let me tell you, said Grandmother Dummer next – that was the strangest thing for Eve to find herself out in the world after such a long time either incarcerated with Adam as his faithful wife or locked up with Mr Brown, pimp and controller of credit – and of women.

It was wonderful, at first, just to walk down the streets and look in the shop windows – even without a coat the freedom was exhilarating.

And Sally, who had nipped into the back entrance of the apartment block on their way out, had pinched a wallet from the pocket of the old man who slept among the dustbins since being rendered homeless by Mr Brown's new South of the River development (in partnership with Frank Blake, obviously).

The wallet had very little in it but there was enough for the friends to go to the Holiday Inn and order a coffee. It came, tipped with lovely frothy milk, and Eve realized what a long time it had been since anyone had waited on *her*.

But it was as she was sipping the divine cappucino that Eve realized she was receiving glances such as she had never in her life received before.

– Don't forget, Grandmother Dummer said, that Eve had been looked at solely by men for practically as long as she could remember. First Adam, then the myriad others who came to Mr Brown's headquarters driven by the Old Adam in men. Eve had forgotten what the glances of women could be like.

And it didn't take her long to understand that she wasn't Eve any longer, not in the original sense, anyway.

Nor was she Lilith – she looked too sleek and well-groomed after all those months with Mr Brown's coiffeur and manicurist and aromatherapist to be the wild wandering wife who first unloosed all the strife into the world.

No – she was simply a harlot.

And the other women didn't like her – or Sally – one little bit.

You'd think they'd feel sisterly, wouldn't you? But not a bit of it. As you'll find, if you should fall into the trap that is the fate of Eve.

But she won't have to be a harlot any longer, will she? we asked.

For surely, even if Sally had been naughty when she forged the Count's signature, they had at least found their freedom?

– Well not exactly, said Grandmother Dummer. At this very moment – and she cocked her head towards the sea, as if she could hear the mermaid singing her pitiless, beautiful song – at this very moment Sally is suggesting that she and Eve share a flat together, you know.

– That'll be all right, then, I said. Elsie looked doubtful, however. If there's a catch anywhere, she'll see it.

– How are they going to pay the mortgage? Grandmother Dummer said quietly. They'll go into business together, of course.

– Yes, Eve was perfectly happy, Grandmother Dummer said when she saw us look up at her doubtfully.

There was the joy, you see, of being able to go where you liked, when you liked.

After doing up the flat – Sally had rather a taste for kitsch, I'm afraid, and practically everything in there was got up to look like something else, so that when you sat on the loo you had the impression you were sitting on the knee of a lady in a crinoline at the court of Queen Charlotte, and when you answered the phone you thought you were involved in a production in a marionette theatre – while Eve went straight for her favourite colour –

– Mauve, we both said.

– Yes, after doing up the flat in every conceivable shade of mauve, from heliotrope and magenta to Old Rose and puce, Eve strolled in the neighbouring flea market and bought knick-knacks or went for coffees and cocktails with the new friends she made on the beat.

Eve and Sally had a holiday – at last – and they went to Venice, where they laughed at the story of Lilith and the divorce lawyer and said how glad they were to be free of all that.

Free of men, paradoxically, for by becoming whores they had freed themselves from the whole chain of stereotypes into which men place and always will place women: it's as if the whore, by being so necessary and so utterly beyond the pale, cancels all the others out immediately.

– But, said Grandmother Dummer, the trouble with mankind, as Pascal said, is that no one can bear to stay alone in his room. And womankind, in particular, hates to be trapped there with a man.

And just as the restlessness that drives the descendants of

Cain and Abe to seek out new adventures, drives men to whores and to war, so Eve, in her search for happiness and fulfilment – and, as the Serpent in the garden knew, sheer inquisitiveness – is destined to stay only a short time in her harlot role.

– And that, said Grandmother Dummer with a sigh, is probably a good thing. But it did seem a shame, really, after escaping from Mr Brown and discovering the enjoyment of an independent life. She wanted to find her children, of course, Grandmother Dummer added hastily – but it was more than that.

It is simply that there is no such thing as a perfectly balanced partnership; and Sally is beginning to get the upper hand.

THE FRIENDS

– You'll probably find, said Grandmother Dummer, that where there are two friends, one will be the practical one and the other the dreamer. Friendships seem to work better that way – a Mary and a Martha, if you like.

And Eve very soon found herself the Martha in her beautiful new friendship with Salome, the red-haired vamp.

Martha, if you remember the Bible, had to do all the washing-up while Mary sat at Jesus's feet and listened to his teaching.

The unfair thing, as you both know, is that Jesus preferred Mary even though she did no housework at all.

It was just like that with Eve and Sally, said Grandmother Dummer as Elsie and I secretly decided that I was the vague, absent-minded one and Elsie had her feet fairly and squarely planted in the world (which is quite true).

Eve found herself having to clean up the flat and fix the meals and make the appointments for gentleman callers, as they used to be called in my own grandmother's day.

And when they came, it was Sally they liked. Anyone

could see that. Sally sat at their feet in a red caftan embroidered with arum lilies and the petals of opium poppies from the Golden Triangle and the rose of Sharon boldly displayed on her left shoulder.

The men thought they were so fascinating in the company of Sally they paid twice over to spend time with her.

Sally chose only managing directors and the heads of consortiums and in return for money she asked for shares – especially if Mr Brown was chief shareholder.

So Sally grew rich and began to bankrupt Mr Brown with her efforts, while Eve, trudging from linen cupboard to dishwasher, made hardly anything at all and was soon taken to be the maid by clients when they came.

Something had to be done about this. Don't you agree, children?

I suppose we were still a little too shocked by the way of life Eve had taken up to agree wholeheartedly.

– Why didn't Eve set out to find her children?

– Couldn't she get a proper job now she was free?

– Oh, she did both, Grandmother Dummer said.

But you remember I told you red-haired Sally was a bit of a dreamer? Well, as you've seen in the episode with the Count, she's inclined to try to make her dreams into reality as well.

In other words she's a hare-brained schemer, which is the worst possible combination for Eve.

When Eve says she wants to find an ordinary, straight-forward job, Sally insists on offering her services as well –

they'll go out as a footman and cook combination (Sally rather fancies cross-dressing, I'm afraid).

They go to all the grandest mansions in the capital (Eve is always the footman; Sally, dressed as a chef, prepares outstanding meals without losing her composure once); and it's only when they get home that Eve realizes she has something in her pocket that definitely wasn't there when they started out.

A silver sugar shifter.

Or a gold-and-tortoiseshell hairbrush and comb.

Or a ring, mounted with diamonds and sparkling like a naughty deed in a dull world.

Eve complains about this thieving, but Sally says these were simply gratuities and there was nowhere else to put them; for Sally likes to change back into her own clothes as soon as they're out of sight – behind a tree, in a hallway will do.

So if the police are called, two men are not to be seen walking back through the streets of the richest part of the capital. Only a man in a dinner jacket (Eve) and his wife, respectable in fur-trimmed coat or floating satin theatre cape, depending on the season.

Things come to a head when, after a dinner at a great ambassadorial residence in the middle of a park, Eve finds something slipped in her pocket that gives her a nasty turn.

It's her engagement ring. The ring Adam gave her all that time ago before they lost their innocence and were condemned forever to live outside the walls of Eden.

A pigeon-egg-sized ruby, worn by the Empress Catherine the Great on the occasions of her famous orgies.

How many weeping men, forced into the bedchamber and lowered on to the recumbent form of the elephantine Empress, has this ring, with its baleful reddish glare, witnessed in their acts of simulated love? And how did the ring get to the ambassadorial residence in the first place?

The first question may be impossible to answer (to the second the obvious answer is that it was sold in the sale of Adam's effects) – yet Eve screams inwardly with rage at the thought, for when she found it missing Adam swore she had lost it herself.

And, if the ring has seen so much unwanted love in its day, why, so has Eve.

So all the way home through the trees and round the side of the pretty ornamental pond, Eve sobs and sobs.

What is the point of life? she howls and gulps – and for a moment it looks as if Lilith is back, because the tops of the trees all moan and gnash their branches and a divorce lawyer, who is at that exact moment negotiating with Mr Brown on the top storey of the apartment block for the room of the late Count von Cruel, finds his tongue grow longer and longer until it sweeps the floor and trips him as he tries to rush out.

What is the point of life, without my husband and children?

◆

– This, said Grandmother Dummer, is a breaking point in Eve's life. Anyone can see that.

And Sally is her best friend. She really wants the best for Eve, and understands they can't go on as Moll Cutpurse for the rest of their days.

– Answer an ad for a job, says Sally. And put another in a different paper offering a reward to whoever brings back your kids.

And Sally generously offers to pay the reward herself. – But mind you don't go for an interview with a Mr Brown, she jokes as Eve goes to pick the harlequin cover from the plastic ivory telephone to do as she is told.

– Did she get the twins back? we asked, when Grandmother Dummer had come in from the kitchen with a cup of tea. We didn't know why, but she didn't look as joyous as she might have done if there was a happy ending in sight.

– Over a thousand children were brought in, Grandmother said in her driest tone, the tone she uses when she's upset and trying to conceal it.

They were all twins, and all ragged and filthy, so that Sally screamed that they'd have to go somewhere else to be identified if it went on like this.

But Sally, if you remember, had a heart of gold.

And Eve – I'm sorry to say this – couldn't tell which, if any of them, were hers.

But they couldn't just throw them back in the street, could they? The mob of urchins – because, really, they looked like something out of *Oliver Twist* – had to be housed somewhere.

This is where Adam comes in.

THE NEW ADAM

— Yes, children, said Grandmother Dummer, but with a twinkle in her eye this time. You are quite right to ask what has happened to Adam. Ex-husbands and fathers do have a way of disappearing, and soon it's as if they never had been.

For Adam, it's been roses all the way.

His wife Brigid's father helped Adam to win the seat for Pontypool and now he's actually in the Cabinet (along with Brigid, his new wife: Brigid is the New Woman who pursues a career while bringing up an adorable pair of tow-headed, blue-eyed children, while Adam is the New Man, photographed with one hand on a diaper and holding in the other a petition from his constituency to re-route the Chunnel under Bradford.

(It was easy for Adam to get a divorce, of course. He told the Court that, when last heard of, Eve had been patrolling the red light district; and Adam was told in private after the immediate granting of a decree nisi that if he had chosen to execute Eve rather than to divorce her, he would have received no more than a suspended three-day sentence for womanslaughter.)

Eve had no settlement, of course. But then, Adam, as you may remember, was bankrupt at the time.

Not now, oh dear no.

Brigid's father is so proud of his son-in-law that he has made over to him his tax-dodge forests on the borders of Scotland and his toxic waste disposal company, with special concessions to dump in the Lebanon.

Adam wears a carnation in his buttonhole – and every time Eve, lying waiting for her next customer in the dolly flat she shares with Sally, sees him on TV with that mauve-pink bloom sitting snugly with a twist of maidenhair fern just under his bright pink face – Adam is so well fed these days, on oysters and pheasant and Queen of Puddings that he has become quite florid – Eve bursts into tears and flicks channels.

The sitcom of Adam and his happy marriage and his burgeoning career is really beginning to get her down.

So, especially as most of the clients want to see themselves reflected in glory in the eyes of Sally, and Eve has less and less inclination to tell each and every man they're the first to turn her on – for men, as we know from Adam First, do like to be told they're first, as if life and even love was one great school race – Eve decides to scan the paper for the small-ads.

She rather fancies joining a film company, getting in at

the bottom, of course, and rising to become a director.

Just as Eve is fantasizing her Biblical epic, which will have a cast ten times larger than a Cecil B. de Mille movie and will have the Serpent stoned to death in the Garden of Eden by a mob of enraged women warriors, fresh from the set of her last multi-grosser *The Dream of St Ursula and the Eleven Thousand British Virgins*, the phone goes.

A male voice says that it has just considered applications – and there are many, the voice implies – for the post as advertised in *The Times*. And the voice would like to fix up a meeting with Eve, among others. Can Eve please come to Transport House at 3 p.m.?

The voice says goodbye and rings off.

– Yes, children, said Grandmother Dummer, Eve had ticked all the ads and applied for every single one of the jobs.

She's a realistic person at heart, and knows she may not find a post with a film company, so, rather like doing the pools, she went for the lot.

The only trouble is, she can't for the life of her remember what a post at Transport House could be.

– I can't tell you how much trouble Eve took with her appearance that afternoon, children. You'd hardly believe, just for an interview for a job, that it could take three hours forty-three minutes of preparation before Eve was ready to step out of the flat, where she had been feeling more and more claustrophobic, recently, into the air of a brighter, fresher future.

Even the mauvey-pinks Eve wore had an innocent,

forward-looking air: cyclamen, in a delightful hat perched jauntily on the side of her head; old-fashioned pinks, to lend an atmosphere of homeliness, tied into the sash of lilac silk at her waist.

No cattleya orchid today, either – for the cattleya, as you may know, is the orchid of sex, the flower of Odette, who broke the heart of Proust's narrator, Swann.

Sadly, Eve decides to go without the fleshy, mauve-pink flower that is usually her corsage – the flower that so resembles that part of her for which men have given their all – and substitutes a rosebud flown down from the virgin valleys of the Upper Hebrides.

At all costs, Eve must be pure, and the amethyst wrist-watch, complete with mini-calculator in misty-pink opal that dangles from her arm, promises – or so she thinks – super-efficiency as well as purity.

Poor Eve.

Adam recognizes her at once, of course, from behind his heavy desk, for which a sizeable rainforest – belonging to his Brazilian colleagues – has been cut down.

And Eve recognizes Adam.

But neither of them has the slightest thing to say to the other.

– But why not? Elsie and I said, when we had recovered from our surprise. For, truth be told, we kept praying Adam and Eve would end up back in Eden together. It didn't matter how many times Grandmother Dummer told us that

that was what all children wanted – just to stay in Eden – and grown-ups wanted to get back there and never could.

– Because Adam knows a tart when he sees one, and he's not going to be taken in by any of Eve's references from the distant days when he first met her as a temp at a big advertising agency – before she moved over to SatelHaven at his request, of course.

He doesn't listen at all when Eve explains how much she wants to work in a fast-moving, streamlined business like his. (She still hasn't the slightest idea why she's in Transport House, but there was a picture of an express train in the hall on the ground floor.)

– No, children, don't take Eve for a fool.

Even as she talks she knows she has only one function as far as Adam is concerned. She might as well have worn the cattleya orchid and told Adam what her charges were, rather than outline the type of salary and job promotion she sought.

And she calculates, quickly, that if she can get Adam home with her, she and Sally will be able to sew him up fairly quickly.

It's not that Eve is vengeful by nature. Just that Adam has his function, too, as far as Eve is concerned; and it's something called being a husband – or, at the very least, paying maintenance for her and the children after the desertion of the family home.

So when Eve looks Adam straight in the eye and says unsmilingly that she'll take him to her place, there's no need for any further discussion over jobs and prospects.

They understand each other perfectly.

– Well, Grandmother Dummer said when we were all sitting together again after a trip to the shingle beach where sometimes we find the strangest flotsam and jetsam washed up (last week it was a coin all encrusted with green, and Elsie's father got excited and said it might be a piece-of-eight, from the journey across the seas of Long John Silver and young Jim Hawkins – but it was only half a crown, and it's a long time, Grandmother said, since she'd seen one of those).

– Well, said Grandmother again. Adam and Eve were very pleased to get into bed together and I'll leave it at that.

And Sally gave a big wink when she saw Eve bring back, instead of a job prospectus or a form to be filled in, a man who looked as if he had a few of those pieces-of-eight or what-have-you on his person. It was time Eve had a lucky break – and here, by the looks of it, it was.

This strange man might even set Eve up in a flat of her own. (Not that Sally wouldn't have missed her, but she'd guessed that Eve was drooping slightly in her own, more domineering, presence.)

Adam and Eve spent all afternoon and most of the evening in Eve's bedroom. And Sally is even more delighted. They'll have a slap-up supper tonight, all right.

– Now you may ask, my dears, why Adam wanted to be with Eve when he had a perfectly good new wife at home.

But the fact is that this had nothing to do with it, and never has.

Men like Adam – and there are many of them – feel free to pay for prostitutes and by so doing they satisfy their lust which they say is greater than women's lust and they satisfy the need to exert financial and physical power over another human being.

What they mustn't expect, though, is to be loved; and Adam is breaking the rules altogether when he asks Eve if she loves him just a little tiny bit.

Adam wants everything. And besides, he can see Eve is quite upset today and perhaps does love him whether she wants to show it or not.

But Eve is furious to be asked this. Indeed, it's the last humiliation: for while Brigid, endlessly filmed and photographed as she loads her blonde cherubs into a station wagon, and tends the walled garden in their new Eden, waits only for the key in the door and the reassurance of Adam's undying love, Adam is actually out with a common whore whom he wants to hear whisper her love to him.

The trouble with Adam is he's used by now to having everything.

But this Eve won't give. And she says in a very cold voice that no, she doesn't love Adam at all, and isn't it time he was thinking of moving on, dearie, as there's others expected in tonight, you know.

Adam is furious. And he makes a very silly mistake.
He leaves without paying.

Now Sally is the kind of good friend that no one really needs. She's as loyal as the Archangel Gabriel and as devoted as the Mary Magdalen, but she does sometimes go a little too far with her life-saving schemes.

And as soon as Adam has left the flat and Eve has revealed his meanness (she's used to it, of course), Sally hits on a plan.

She goes into the next room, lifts the Pierrot outfit from the wall-phone, and rings *The Daily Grope*.

But Eve and Sally are both out of work now and starving.

After all, they should have known that Adam First, amongst his many other city interests, was also the proprietor of *The Daily Grope*.

The heating has been cut off, and the mild weather has suddenly turned Arctic cold.

Having sold all their clothes, they spend the day in bed, under a ragged eiderdown.

It's then that Sally suddenly remembers that, ages ago, she booked the ad offering a reward for the finder of Eve's children.

And – really – when they least need it, a thousand ragamuffins turn up. How are they to feed them? Where will they all sleep?

– My dears, finished Grandmother Dummer, the only thing we can look for here to save the situation is an Act of God. Literally, a miracle.

– I don't know, she went on with that slightly naughty look she had, if you'd call Lilith an Act of God.

– But – it's worth remembering – Lilith and Eve have become good pals since Adam gave Eve the big goodbye.

They often meet for coffee, and have their hair done at the same place: Eve to look beautifully like a French *marquise* (which seems to be all the rage these days, since *The Dangerous Liaisons*), and Lilith to get all the grit and boulders and thunderclaps washed out after one of her great climatic safaris across the world.

And Lilith freezes the Garden of Eden.

Pears drop like great icicles from the sunny, south-facing wall.

The children wake glued to their pillows with cold.

The school is frozen inside its main door, so the staff stand entranced with the cold like the staff in *Sleeping Beauty*.

Surely, Lilith has cursed Adam and his new wife with her terrible cold snap.

The children are at home all day, and we know Adam doesn't like that. He even begins dreaming of Eve and wondering where she is, when the fifth snowball hits him fair and square in the chest.

Lilith sends the worst air crashes, the most terrible train collisions, the most fatal and impossible car concertinas along the motorways.

Death and ice reigns for the Minister of Transport. His resignation is called for: how dare he stay in the Garden of Eden while the people suffer and die?

Adam resigns.

Disgusted and bored, Brigid leaves. (All the pipes have been frozen for weeks and the conservatory has cracked so that all the tropical flowers have died. The servants have long ago returned to the sunny climes from which they came.)

– And so you see, children, one day, when a fresh fall of snow has buried house and garden almost completely, and frost marks out the eyebrows of the upper windows with its scintillating brush-strokes, Eve arrives home, to Eden.

Only this time, she brings all the children, and Sally, with her.

The screams and broken Action Man bits, the three-legged My Little Ponies, the constant jarring thump screech from robot radios turn Eden, in Adam's sorrowing eyes, into a Hieronymus Bosch-like vision of Hell.

MADONNA

– Oh, you can't miss the look on her face, says Grandmother Dummer. We're standing in the little church and, for the first time, we see the Virgin as she really is: mournful, preoccupied with the burden of love taken on in the name of the whole world; suffering and pain etched in the fine stained-glass that brings the sunlight in through the window and turns her hair daffodil yellow, her robe the blue of the sea.

All the world over, she is worshipped and revered. And, where the sea is bluest, so is the worship all the more devout.

In whitewashed squares, where men sit idling on the cobbles by grubby café doors – entrances to Hell with their black stench of frying oil and a greasy curtain of beads – the women are hidden away for fear of loss of honour, and the Holy Virgin rules over the minds and souls of the fishermen and tillers of the field. In the lap of her blue gown, childhood returns with the force of the plaster images that hang on every wall, the face of the Madonna staring sadly and soulfully down on the infant at the breast.

And in Ireland, where the sea is grey, the tears of the Madonna fall with the steady patter of the rain, as the Troubles go on, as brother fights brother, and all in the name of the son of the Holy Mother of God.

It didn't take Eve long to find that the new life awaiting her when she returned to Eden with her brood wasn't what she had hoped for at all – not here, at least. If she went out to the supermarket, the children were arrested for theft and misbehaviour – but no provision had been made for them while she spent the money hard-earned with Sally in the days of their joint business venture.

If Eve and Adam – and Sally and the children – went to a riverside pub or off to the country for a day's outing, as often as not the women were made to perch with the children in bleak little rooms and eat baby food while Adam was served with his foaming tankard at the bar.

If Eve wanted to leave her children for a part of the day and supplement her income there was no chance of that. Crèches and kindergartens, long-promised, always failed to materialize – and help, as feeding all the children and paying the electricity and gas in Eden already amounted to a hefty sum – was far too expensive.

On top of all that, neighbours jealous of their temporary ease – for so many, after all, were not housed at all; and Eden, for all that it had a hole in the roof and the porch looked as if it was about to break off altogether, so cracked and damp-ridden had it become – neighbours, as I say, started to report Adam to the police for child abuse and anything else they could think up.

There must be something wrong, they said, with a family that has so many children. And what does the husband do, anyway? Hangs around the house all day, doesn't he?

And as their tongues wagged, and Eden began to pull out in the shape of a bunioned foot, with the chimneys listing into laces and the staircase like a great leather tongue down which all the children rushed a hundred times a day – Eve decided it was time to go to a country where the Madonna would not be taken in vain.

To a country where the sea is blue, blue as the eyes of the Virgin, as she gazes down at Baby Jesus on her knee.

Here Grandmother Dummer paused, and we knew she was thinking that it must be hard for us to believe that Eve could go back to being a Virgin again, when only recently she had been so very much the opposite.

– But, she told us, it's perfectly possible. Because, as I'll try to explain, men cannot accept to themselves that their mother is anything other than a virgin from beginning to end of her life.

This is stronger by far than the Oedipus complex – which was invented, after all, by a man who knew the power of jealousy and rivalry, but did not understand that Oedipus had never any desire for his mother – only the desire that his mother had never been impregnated by any human agency at all.

It goes back, if you like, to the days I told you of – when nymphs brought forth children after being visited by the wind – or after bathing in a spring or a stream. In those days, boys and girls didn't even know how to have sex, and had to be instructed, as the poet Longinus tells us, in the case of the shepherd-boy Daphnis and the fair Chloe, by their old nurse, in the practicalities of the act.

You can see how it is, in the lands where the Madonna reigns supreme, the Catholic countries where mariolatry is the faith of faiths.

– You could say, I suppose, said Grandmother Dummer, reflecting (though she knew, very likely, that all this was way above our head) – you could say, in those countries where boys and girls must not make love before marriage, and where the harlot is the only alternative, along with the Scandinavian tourist, these days, to burning in the midday sun, that sexual repression is one of the main causes of the reverence accorded to the Madonna.

To put it another way, if you can't have the local girls, then no one has ever had your mother, either. All men in those climes are celibate, sinning and confessing sons of Mary.

And in the countries where Protestants rule the roost, the funny part is that the mother is sacred, still – although the freedom of women is a great deal more pronounced.

– But honestly, says Grandmother Dummer, can you imagine a man boasting of the amount of sexual partners his mother has enjoyed?

Maybe – in the days of the god Pan – if he really was the offspring of Penelope after she fucked all her suitors in the wait for Odysseus to return home – but here Grandmother

Dummer broke off and burst out laughing.

– Anyone would think I had been alive myself then, she said (although we knew perfectly well she had). And no one will ever know if there really was a time when the earth mother's sexual appetite was a matter of pride for her children. Even if we suspect so.

– Certainly, Grandmother Dummer added with a sigh, the all-devouring mother of insatiable lusts is the other side of the Virgin, chaste and sorrowing single parent.

And Eve, as she packed up and left Eden – which, shoe as it had become, now stood on its uppers among a desert of waste and broken glass and all the detritus of the slum lands surrounding it – was to show both sides of her nature, as she travelled in the realms of Our Lady of the Cross.

– Not that Adam was blameless, either, said Grandmother Dummer. And she sighed again, quite loudly this time.

You see – and here she took us both by the hands and led us to the French window that opens out on to the grassy garden with the slice of blue that is the sea beyond – the waves go on coming in and the tides come in and out, and yet neither Adam nor Eve could find any peace with each other, or in themselves.

– Why? Elsie and I wanted to say, but somehow the sight of the ocean, with its strict rules as it meets the sky, and the wild little white-capped waves dancing about within the confines allotted to them, made us keep quiet. It was as if, perhaps, we knew that some things were too mysterious and unfathomable for us – as indeed they must be, if even Grandmother Dummer was perplexed by men and women and their eternal strife.

– If Adam could have been more like Eve, and if she could have been more like him, Grandmother Dummer mused, it might have turned out all right.

But Adam wasn't a bit like Eve; and the more she became Madonna, the less chance there was, obviously, of any twin understanding growing up between them.

For one thing – as Eve saw after a few weeks in Eden – Adam was beginning to shrink.

It was very gradual at first, and Adam did everything he could to combat it. When his jeans, hung out in the weedy Garden of Eden, where stray cats roamed and kids had made an adventure playground that was more of a Death Row enterprise scheme, billowed on the line and then promptly fell from Adam when he stepped into them, Eve accused him of going on a secret diet. (The truth of the matter was that she was herself secretly jealous of Adam's slim figure. But Madonnas must never express a desire for anything so wicked and selfish as a shape.) And if Adam wasn't fasting, then exactly what *was* he doing, to keep so very much in trim?

Eve knew the answer to this in her heart of hearts. But she couldn't bear to admit it to herself.

After all, they were a real family now.

There was Lilith's brood, fostered and loved by Eve, who put down a thousand bowls of muesli each morning and stuffed the washing-machine with a score of pants and dungarees on the hour every hour.

There were her own children –

– Yes, we said, for we had been longing, also secretly, to hear what had happened to Abe and Cain. What are they like now? Were they happy when Eve found them again? Do they like being in their real home, where they can climb trees?

– Oh yes, Grandmother Dummer smiles.

Eve gives them all she can, to make up for their deprived early years. (She feels guilty all the time now she is Madonna. Simply by bringing the kids into the world she has crucified them, on the cross of her appalling desire to be a person in her own right.)

Eve-Madonna has accepted that it's all her fault.

She knows she only tried to earn her living after Adam went off, broke, with Brigid the Ice Princess.

She knows she only tried to please Adam, with her lovely new nightie and suggestions of a weekend in Paris or Venice, leaving the children behind.

And she knows she is receiving her punishment here on earth, which consists of muesli every day, and a centre parting and long hair, and smocks that give no indication that anything other than an angry, accusing baby is crouching in there waiting to be born.

Poor Madonna! No wonder she longs, at least, for the

reverence of Latin countries, the men crossing themselves as they help her cross the road with her enormous, ego-crazed brood.

Abe and Cain, Grandmother Dummer says, are spoiled in order to make up for the lack of a proper Madonna in their lives from the very first.

With money lent by Sally – and with the proceeds from the ruby ring Adam gave Eve in what seems another incarnation, it's so long ago – Eve buys the boys real miniature Bugattis and cellular telephones and airguns with telescopic sights and cine-cameras with boom and zoom, and a health pension plan for psychoanalysts from the age of seventeen for life.

When the boys kick Eve, she kisses the bruise in front of them, so they can see that even the wounds they inflict are holy.

They are loved. Utterly loved.

– But, and again Grandmother Dummer sighed dramatically, it's too late, I'm afraid. They hate Eve and that's all there is to it.

Out in the garden, where they have kicked down the wall where Eve's fine peach and nectarines once grew, and where all the other wild kids from the slums crowd in, they let any hobbledehoy shout Son of a Bitch! and they cheer and crow with cruel joy, for they know Eve can hear them, from the conservatory with the broken glass roof where she hangs out their handwash silk Armani shirts, all three hundred and sixty-five of them, so they can change once a day into something soft to the skin.

And Eve knows they know. She is a bitch; and these are her sons. She neglected them. And now she will pay the price. So, children, I'm sorry to say that Abe and Cain have not turned out very well, after all. Abe has charm, but he's a drifter really. It doesn't look as if he'll keep Eve in her old age. And Cain – the amount of times you see Eve-Madonna waiting in the ante-rooms of gaols for the twice-quarterly visit to their murderer sons ...

Poor Eve. At least she knows now for real that she's entirely to blame.

– However, Grandmother Dummer says when we've had time to decide that we will never, ever fall for being Madonna, however nice that woman in St Ives seemed, with her triplets in a troilist push-chair and a gang of toddlers in tow too – however, Eve isn't allowed just to work and scrub and suffer and weep for all the bleeding humanity to which she has given birth.

Oh no, she must go on living in the real world – for that is what Eden, unfortunately, has now become.

Eve weeps silently at night when she peels off her smock and sees the hump, grey with stretch-marks, creased again by the strained elastic of her gargantuan tights; the humpy lump that once had been her waist.

Her huge breasts catch her tears and for a split second the greater globules seem to quiver in sympathy with the smaller, evanescent pearls of salty grief.

Yet – people tell Eve she is so lucky.

There's nothing like a big family, says the woman in the sweet shop, who has got used to a thousand liquorice sticks going in one shopping expedition, and has a van come round to collect the pennies and take them to the bank.

Go on, have another, joke the mothers of other kids who come to play. And they exchange looks, like addicts who will go on destroying themselves rather than change their ways.

Room for one more inside.

So it's when Eve becomes pregnant with Seth (she doesn't bother to get it confirmed by the doctor any more: the adjustable band on the dungarees just lets itself out with a resigned sigh) that she really notices how terribly small Adam has become.

And she has to confront the necessity of an immediate move away from home – even if it means jogging about on a donkey, in search for a room at the inn.

Eve is being betrayed by a rapidly dwindling man.

– Now, as you'll remember, children, said Grandmother Dummer, Adam makes quite a habit of getting off with other women when Eve is having a baby. It's something of a tradition, I fear: in the West at least. And Adam has a lot to learn from those African tribes where the men practise the *couvade* – that is, the man goes right through the symptoms of pregnancy and when the time comes for the baby to be born he goes off to lie in his hut and really does suffer labour pains in sympathy.

None of this for Adam, as you may well imagine.

And for a time, on being accused by Eve of getting smaller, he easily turns it round and tells Eve what an absolute mountain *she* has become (which, of course, she has).

But after a while there does seem to be a big discrepancy between the Adam of the days when Eden was like an advertisement for private enterprise in the headiest years of the Age of Money – and all brought home by Adam, who seemed to grow larger and ruddier with every rise in profits, twice the girth at the time of a successful takeover – and the Adam of today, who has had to creep off to Harrods Prep School outfitters to replace those jeans now as big on him as a patch of summer sky.

Is it because Adam hasn't been able to get a look in with Eve? Is he left out, in the equation that is Madonna's, where the sum total of the offspring more than cancels the power of the father and denies the poor square a root?

Yes it is.

For whereas Eve in the early blushing days of marriage to Adam, when in richness, in poorness had meant to her an effort to reassure her husband that the birth of those two bouncing boys had in no way staunched her eager desire to love and fuck her stallion, her brilliant groom –

– Well, as I was saying, Grandmother Dummer said, when a neighbour had called and left a bag of rock cakes on the kitchen table in the little farmhouse, had been thanked and had duly left –

– It wasn't suitable for your ears anyway, said Grandmother Dummer when we tried to get her back to Eve's wiles and lures to her husband in the first flush of their conjugal life.

– I'll just say that when Eve was poor she got her advice from magazines left lying about in the ladies' hairdressers where she was sometimes lucky enough to find work pulling hairs from crimplene chair covers and rinsing basins where the dandruff cases had received their treatment.

And when she was rich, the editors of the most important glossy magazines in the Western world came to her and told her secrets of love, pressed ampoules of the horn of rhinoceros and ginseng suppositories on Eve, to help her keep her sheikh, her Arabian knight of a husband.

Now, she has no desire whatever to read or listen to any advice on the retaining of a spouse whose use is minimal.

And if she does weep sometimes when she sees her own haunches in the mirror last thing, and envisages only a coating of golden breadcrumbs and a fine glaze of honey, cinnamon and cloves on the expanse of pink flesh, before realizing she sees herself and is dreaming up the ultimate sin of self-cannibalism –

If she does cry from time to time, says Grandmother Dummer, mostly she's looking pretty pleased with herself and secretive – like that picture of her you have in your book on Renaissance art; or like the Virgin just up the hill in the church.

Oh no, no flies on Madonna.

She despises Adam now; and that, no doubt, is why Adam is going down so fast, like an inflatable toy after a children's party.

She doesn't need him for anything. That's the terrible fact.

For when Eve wanted Seth to be born, she asked Sally to go and draw off some sperm for her and freeze it in the sperm bank until she was absolutely ready to wash out another muesli bowl and get recycled nappies from the Greens who stand huddled on corners in the streets of Eden, with their banners proclaiming the urgent need to save the world.

– Just show him one of Cain's porno videos, Eve says when Sally asks mildly how a wizened little dwarf like Adam can possibly be expected to get it up.

– Tell him about the time we were in old Mr Brown's brothel – anything. For Eve and Sally both know – and most women learn – that men are horribly excited to hear about the sexual exploits of women together. And once a year, on Adam's birthday, Eve and Sally undress and make love with each other in a bath of rose petals gathered from the wilderness that was once Eve's famous rose garden.

For with children, how can you keep a neat garden growing?

It's hard enough to bribe them to get out of the house for the short time the 'show' takes. Poor Adam, so tiny and wasted that the sight of Madonna's piggy thighs straddled by Sally in a bowler hat and whip is really the high spot of his year, has to be contented with that. (He complains he doesn't feel he's the new baby's real father; but then he wasn't much good with Abe and Cain either, if you remember, so Eve says she simply couldn't give a damn.)

– I hardly need, says Grandmother Dummer, to spell out Adam's reaction to finding himself so appallingly neglected by the woman who had once been his bride, his chattel, his mistress and his muse.

It's the most obvious in-house revenge you can think of – and Adam is so small by now, anyway, that he can't go any further than the precincts of the house which his ex-wife Brigid paid for and which is now falling apart since the stocks and shares that held it up have been pulled out. *Kaput*, poor Adam can be heard muttering to himself, as he sees another field of damp-rot mushrooms blossom in the room that was once his power study, a couple more floorboards sagging and falling in the dressing-room where once he kept those white Tom Wolfe suits that wowed the secretaries in the lobby of the House of Commons.

– Oh God, what shall I do? What will become of me?

– Now we know, says Grandmother Dummer, before Elsie and I can become too sorry for Adam's predicament, three things.

First, that a Madonna has her hands full bringing up her

flock and has no time for the self-indulgent moaning of a man who ought to find a job, even if he has been thrown out of every club and institution in the country since his scandal as a minister.

Second, as I told you before, men do have a way of disappearing altogether when a baby's on the way. Or if not ...

Third, they go off with the wife's best friend.

– Well, didn't I tell you, Grandmother Dummer said in a resigned tone, as if all the wickedness in the world had been spread in front of us and now she was sorry for it.

But Sally was terribly bored in Eden, you know. House-work is just not her thing; and lately she has come to feel more and more a handmaid to Eve, whose mystic Madonna expression as she nears the end of term with Seth is grating on her nerves like anything.

Besides which, Sally is a competitive type, as you remem-ber. Why should Eve have landed this husband and this home and be the proud mother of all these kids when all Sally has is the spare room that the central heating doesn't quite reach, with the single sofa-bed Lilith sent as a present – double-edged perhaps – to Eve when she moved back into Eden.

Why should she? When she's been so generous to Eve – and Adam too, for that matter – supplying them with much of the original furniture sold at the sale to clients of

Sally's in her harlot days and taken in return for favours granted.

What's in it for Sally?

And soon, as the apple blossom comes out in the wilderness of an orchard where once the orchids grew in the tropical greenhouse and the puma (long since running wild in Devon and terrorizing would-be rural retreaters) once prowled, as hungry for the lovely Eve as its master – Sally starts to dream of a home and husband of her own.

Yes – she can see it.

The cottage has roses round the door and lupins and hollyhocks in the front garden. The thatch keeps her and her happy, lucky husband as snug as two bugs in a rug right through the long, snowy winter.

In summer they take the children to the sea, which is just visible from the back garden and they play on the beach with their friendly labrador.

Sally turns pale and her dreams grow worse. In the orchard the wild garlic smells like the million candle-lit *ratatouilles* she and her wedded spouse will eat when the little ones are tucked up safe and sound under the eaves.

Oh dear!

– Yes, said Grandmother Dummer, I'm afraid it took Madonna a long time to notice anything was going wrong with her marriage – or that's how the marriage guidance counsellor put it, anyway; and if both Adam and Madonna looked surprised to hear what they had described as a marriage at all, then they were careful not to show it.

(It wasn't just on emotional grounds, actually. Tax concessions and single person's allowances would have been taken from them if they admitted to the fact that, after Brigid left, they had never got round to remarrying.)

After all, Adam and Eve *are* the real marriage. Lilith can't be counted either: she's the mad woman in the attic and Eve is the lovely, submissive Jane Eyre.

Before she became the Old Woman who lives in a Shoe, of course.

– Anyway, says Grandmother Dummer, the marriage guidance counsellor says she thinks it would be a very good idea if Adam and Eve had a little breather away from each other. They're very much under each other's feet at home all day, aren't they? There's time yet, before Seth is born, for Adam to take a brief holiday, or – and here the social worker clears her throat – or to find gainful employment. Even if it meant moving his family – they'll feel ever so much better if –

Stupid woman!

Eve wakes one morning and she realizes Adam has gone, by the lack of the very slight indentation in the enormous bed where Madonna lies with her litter, the number seeming to proliferate by the hour, so that children swarm on the quilt, fill the duvet and pile high on the bolsters – on many occasions nearly crushing Adam to death while they play.

Adam has gone.

*

Eve can hear the wedding bells ring out, as she lies giving suck to Seth; and she remembers the last time. And she decides she won't let it happen again. She must go. Adam must come with her. To the blue skies, where Eve-Madonna will seem to all the men to have stepped down from the triptych in the church in the piazza, radiating miracles and heaven-sent love and compassion.

– You may ask, said Grandmother Dummer, why Eve would want to take Adam with her wherever she goes.

And you would be right to ask – but, you see, a woman with children is at a very great disadvantage unless there is a man about. And Eve has no intention of going back on the streets this time, or taking up part-time work to feed the army of kids.

(Yes, what is she going to do for money? Well, as I said, she has some of the proceeds of that ruby ring put aside. And it's so much cheaper to live in the South of Italy, where the women dance the tarantella for a whole week without falling down and the men cheer and clap and pass round the wine. Or Spain, where the bullfighters will bow and sweep the road with their broad-brimmed hats when the Holy Maria, glass tear frozen on her cheek, is carried by in the procession on a silver bier.)

Without Adam, Eve would be no more than a bitch that has whelped too often and too lustfully. Drown the bitch and her mongrel pups!

Eve bides her time. She hears the patter of confetti as

Sally and Adam leave the fashionable church in the centre of town; and she smells the orange blossom in Sally's bridal wreath as it floats down towards her through the stinking cesspit that the streets round Eden have become.

Eve suffers every humiliation.

Sally and Adam become a well-seen, upwardly mobile couple and with the rest of Sally's earnings they buy a house in a conservation village. Many of Eve's children prefer staying with Sally and Adam because it's more comfortable there and Sally doesn't make them eat up their boiled eggs and soldiers.

Eve grits her teeth in rage when they come back from the weekends in the house built at the end of the reign of Victoria for large families with hypocrites and patriarchs at the head; and she has to pretend to smile happily when she's shown the polaroids they've taken.

Of Adam plumper and larger than he's been for some time. Look at that designer sweater! Yes, Ma, he's got a job in an advertising agency. They're going to buy a cottage in Wales, him and Sally!

Of Sally in the well-tended garden of her new Eden, squinting at the camera in a devil-may-care mood.

Eve wanders in her wilderness of an orchard and shouts aloud to the heavens in her rage. And Lilith, hearing her, rumbles in the worst thunderstorm in living memory, uproots trees as if they were no more than nettles growing in her path, and strikes the whole of the pretty, well-conserved village where Adam and Sally live.

What can have happened to the weather? cry the fearful inhabitants. Save us, please!

But Lilith, who is a force of Nature, is acting now on Nature's behalf. For all the poisons unleashed into the atmosphere when Adam was a minister in the Cabinet, Lilith sends a trumpet blast of all the 'natural' disasters which so afflict the rest of the world, but never the smug neo-Victorians in their villas.

A typhoon lifts Sally up and has her dangling like an escaped gas balloon miles over the roofs of the city.

A monsoon drowns the pretty gardens and carries a sludge of marigolds and Sweet William down the gutters and clogs the sewage system, where the rats, finding a new way to climb out as the sweepers try to clear the garden debris, run in packs in the streets and spread plague.

And finally an earthquake is sent by Lilith and the whole fast-gentrifying area is swallowed up.

So, late one night and dripping wet, with festering rat bites and a twisted ankle from falling down the rapidly-widening crack outside his house, Adam appears at the gates of Eden. Come in, says Eve; rubs him down and gives him a sandwich; and off to bed with him.

*

The next day, in a caravan with seven trailers, Madonna and her family leave for sunnier climes.

◆

It took us a bit of time to understand from Grandmother Dummer that the sand we played on in Cornwall, with its damp, brownish colour and its unexpected pools where water lay in pockets like thrown-away handkerchiefs, in no way resembled the thronged beaches of the Mediterranean. There, it seemed, all the Madonnas stretched themselves out in great black tents along the water's edge, while their children ran in and out of the folds. Here, on this jagged tip of England, as we could see, only one or two children seemed to belong to any one family; and there was more attention paid to the dogs, which came often in packs with their devoted owners.

Until you've seen the Latin love of children, Grandmother Dummer said, you won't know what parental love is.

The *bambini* are allowed to stay up late into the night and are kissed and petted instead of being sent off to bed.

The ice-creams are so famously good that every child knows before its alphabet the different flavours of the Neapolitan, and the Florentine, and the Granita dark grainy coffee ices.

And when they run in the sea no one cares if they pee.

– Of course, Grandmother Dummer said hastily – as if these revelations were far more shocking than the information on the practices of adults in love and money, the sea does get very polluted as a result.

But, to begin with at least, Madonna and her brood are perfectly and idyllically happy in their commune – yes, that's what it is – by the sea in Italy's toe, Calabria.

(You may ask how the commune works. Well, it's not as communal as it sounds. Madonna, who can pay small sums to her peasant helpers, does just that; and the thick pasta and tomato sauce that is the staple fare of the southern Italians is brought them every day on the beach, along with a great jug of EST! EST! EST!, which happens to be Adam's favourite wine.) Strangely enough, they feel as if they are living on equal terms with Giulietta and Maria and Nina – but never mind: for the time being, at least, everyone is happy (though it's no good Adam's remembering his days of grandeur in Eden when a different chef for each day of the week produced his or her national dishes) and asking for gnocchi or fegato alla Veneziana. No, it's macaroni as thick as a baby's arm and a rough ragu with strong-tasting oil; or it's nothing.

Of course there *are* snags, apart from Seth's sunburn (he has a very fair skin, as if to make up for Cain's dark brow and Abe's rather irritating mop of pastoral brown-sheep curls).

The main problem is that Adam simply isn't getting any bigger.

However much he eats of pure carbohydrate – which makes Madonna double her weight in the first week, so the Italian men clear a great ditch for her in the sand to spread her mammoth thighs and her bottom the size of a dinghy at least – Adam seems if anything to be getting smaller again.

*

– Is he unhappy that he's left Sally? Elsie wonders. For, like me, she had come to like Sally and was sorry she'd been thrown on the scrapheap just because nature, in the shape of Lilith at its worst, and of Madonna, at its most Promethean, had decided there was no place for her. Perhaps Adam would fatten up again if Sally could come and live there as well?

– No, said Grandmother Dummer, as we thought of the witch fattening up Hansel in the cage in her cottage in the woods. And we couldn't help thinking of Hansel's finger as he poked a chicken bone through the bars instead, to bamboozle the old witch.

Madonna became in our minds a huge witch, the size of our own cottage, and with bars all round from which Adam would never be able to escape.

Many men, we were told, had that feeling when they became subsumed by maternity and all its restricting mess of gurgling, demanding human life. They felt the mother was a prison and not a wife any longer; and many tunnelled their way out as soon as they could.

As we have seen, though, Adam hasn't got a hope in hell of starting a new and dignified life – not the way he's going down, like a cheese soufflé that just didn't quite rise when taken from the oven.

He'd be laughed out of town.

And this, unfortunately, is beginning to happen to Madonna as she walks – or sails – in her vast towelled robe through the little village to the beach.

Laughter. The first man to cry 'bambino!' at Adam as he trots along in the rear, desperately trying to keep up, is shushed by the elders at their perennial trades in the unending glare of the Mafiosi-owned sun.

But then a cheeky boy echoes the call. And then they shout it —

Bambino! Bambino!

And that night Adam, as if he couldn't hold out any longer against the irresistible need to join the family of Madonna, comes shyly up to her as she's putting an army of bronzed gypsy children to bed; and asks if he can come right up close.

— Yes, said Grandmother Dummer. It was bound to happen. And it's very often the only way a man can deal with the terrible change in his life a family can bring about. If there's no escape, that is, or if he's infantile at heart, which most men — after their upbringing with their own mother Madonna — inevitably are.

Adam lies in the arms of Madonna and he drinks the milk from her breast.

He is small now, smaller than Seth; and Madonna has to be especially protective of him when the boys play — for fear Cain decides to play an Oedipus trick, or the others simply kick him too hard. (In fact, Adam is more trying than a small child, for he is more truculent than the others when it comes to having to share the love and attention of the Mother of them All.)

— Oh dear, said Grandmother Dummer, when Elsie and I

looked at each other in wonderment. You're asking why Adam was OK with Sally, and with Brigid, but not with Eve. Well, I can't answer that; but it's with the real mate that things seem to go so very wrong.

Madonna is as kind as anything to the new addition to her family.

But the trouble is, she is now a woman on her own in a Latin country; and an unpleasant-looking man with curled mustachios has taken to paying a call in the evening when everyone is asleep but the powerless and jealous Adam.

Madonna has no need of a brigand; or of having her brood sent off to beg on the streets of Naples.

So – once more, and at dead of night to avoid detection – she decamps, making for the East.

– Can you imagine, Grandmother Dummer said, what it is like to find yourself in a village in the mountains of Kerkyra – that's Corfu; but don't get any tourist nonsense into your heads; the village of Doukades where poor Madonna turns up after hitching a lift with her brood on the ferry from Brindisi to Patras, only given her on the understanding that seven of her children swab the decks with seven mops, to be replaced every seven hours by seven more –

– can you imagine, as I was saying, what it is to find yourself in the house of a bad-tempered old woman, who tells you what to do and whom you have to obey day and night for fear of losing your right to a hard and lumpy bed in the room where the cock crowing underneath in the freezing dawn wakes you before you've had time to fall asleep?

– No, said Grandmother Dummer; unless you feel you're already in the house of such a bad-tempered old woman. And she laughed suddenly in a way that made Elsie and me think she was a witch, perhaps, underneath it all, and poor Madonna might walk in any moment and be given all the hard, thankless tasks about the house to do.

– Madonna had to marry the Greek fisherman she met on the beach in the west of the island, said Grandmother Dummer.

I mean, what else could she do? She had nowhere to live, and the money from the sale of the ruby ring had gone down and down, so that it wouldn't buy more than a few postcards of the blue, blue sea and an *ouzo*.

Adam was accepted as a retard, or a misfit, of which there are many in those poor villages where interbreeding and lack of medical care produces fools and simpletons who are given a good deal more tolerance than they are in our big, tense cities.

The trouble was, Madonna had to live with the fisherman's mother. Yes, that's the rule out there; and after the nuptial feast which went on for three days and three nights and all the octopus and rice was eaten and all the retsina (which tastes of pine furniture, you know, children; I don't think you would like it at all) had been drunk, Madonna found herself in that lumpy bed with Nicos – whose party trick was to lay a live fish on the kitchen table and put a cigarette in its mouth, so it appeared to be puffing out smoke with its dying breaths – and a mother-in-law so ferocious that she started her day by granting her son's wife a good beating, before a breakfastless five-mile donkey-ride to the olive groves and a meagre hillside plot owned by the family.

Poor Madonna! And, meanwhile, poor Adam and the rest of the little ones, who were consigned to sleep with the animals under the house and were woken by the stench of the donkey or a sudden angry kick from a mule.

Here was the dream of Mediterranean harmony and happiness! (Of course, it suited Adam. As a man, albeit a tiny one, he was able to sit in the kafeneion all day long, nursing a cup of Turkish coffee and smoking a Greek cigarette. In these countries all the heavy work is women's work. And as for the real children, they too are on their hands and knees eighteen hours a day, picking fallen olives from the ground and making bundles of faggots and weed for the livestock at the end of a working day.)

When Madonna was half-way up the side of a hill where a rich expatriate had ordered a villa to be built – for the women must carry the cement and the bricks, in towering piles on their heads, up thorny paths in the blistering noonday heat – she decided to get out as fast and smoothly as she could.

– She decided, children – and here Grandmother Dummer looked a little ashamed, as if once again we were unsuitable recipients of her confidences –

Eve decided to be Eve once more.

Of course, it meant leaving some of the children behind. But Adam was there, after all, to keep an eye on them.

Elsie laughed derisively at this.

– I know, I know, said Grandmother Dummer. But isn't Madonna by now too burdened down? No better than a beast of the field, I'd say. (And often she longs to change places with the ass, which doesn't get the sharp edge of its mother-in-law's tongue half of the time. Indeed, the mule, child of the donkey with a horse, can be heard to be pretty unpleasant to its mother, for a horse is a more distinguished parent than a donkey. But that's to stray from the point.)

– The point, children, is that Madonna decides to go to India – and Malaysia and Thailand – and as the Madonna isn't exactly a revered figure in these countries, it seems a handful of children is as much as she can risk.

She is sure, you see, that a Maharajah will offer her untold riches as soon as she sets foot in his lost magic kingdom; and then she will bring the fortune back to the village of Doukades and Adam will grow big and strong on this new injection of capital – and they will build a villa of their own, overlooking the sea.

Foolish Madonna!

The journey is long and arduous, especially as, penniless as they are, Eve and Cain and Abe and Seth have to travel strapped to the side of a beast, disguised as icons in packing cases being taken on a heritage trail back to Constantinople after their theft in the Middle Ages and transportation to the Basilica of St Spiridon in Corfu.

TV cameras follow the little procession as it climbs mournfully through the scrub and boulders of Turkey and Asia Minor.

But – at last – when Eve and her family are almost as flattened and dried out as the icons they are accompanying – they arrive at the portals of the East.

Here Grandmother Dummer paused.

– The East was a mystery to Eve-Madonna and her brood, she said. They were treated with kindness, but it was just as if they didn't exist, you know.

They slept in a snake-temple; and Seth learnt how to stroke the pythons and hold them out for visiting Americans and Australians to see.

Abe was in charge of the tortoises that sleep the millennia away in the ivory tower-temple of Penang.

Madonna fried sea-lice in a café where the juke-box blared

day and night and monkeys jumped down out of the palm trees into her hair.

There wasn't a maharajah to be seen anywhere. All the rich Singaporean businessmen found Madonna far too large for their tastes (and one of them, thinking Seth was a white monkey from the Upper Volta imported as a delicacy, tried to eat his brains in the time-honoured way – that is, tying the living meal under a table with a round hole in the surface and taking a knife to slice open the top of the brain).

By now, they are all in rags, and several times, on the banks of the Ganges, they are mistaken for corpses and tossed on to a pyre.

It's time to go home.

– And, said Grandmother Dummer, that's just what they did. It took them a long time – at first, that is – but by the time they'd crossed the sub-continent of India by elephant (as extras in an epic which ended up on the cutting-room floor) and flown over Turkey on a prayer mat lent by the chief caliph after one look at Madonna's impressive girth –

They found themselves at Athens airport, where it was easy to stow away in the forward WCs of a jumbo jet bound for the West.

– And what about Adam? And the rest of the family? Elsie and I said together. I suppose we were still at that stage where to throw away one single doll seems murderous. Yet Grandmother Dummer shook her head and said we must learn to live with the ebb and flow of people in the story of Adam and Eve.

– They're just a nuclear family now, she said. The way things are meant to be. (We looked rather worried at this. But Grandmother Dummer was trying to suppress a smile.)

– The only trouble, she told us when we asked what happened to this nuclear family next, is that events have overtaken Adam and Eve.

Eden, so long neglected by its owners, and with no rates or community charge paid, has indeed become a community.

In fact, it's a squat, Grandmother Dummer said. And there's no room for the recently re-integrated Adam – growing by the minute, now he's back on home ground without Lilith's plague of brats – and his new family.

– And how does Eve solve it this time? says Grandmother Dummer. When Adam can't raise a mortgage to save his soul?

Why, Grandmother Dummer says, she tells lies.

COURTESAN

Lies, said Grandmother Dummer, are what you have already been brought up on, my poor girls. And the lies will go on until the day you die, unless you really take care to identify a lie when you hear one, that is.

Elsie and I exchanged glances, but decided to keep quiet. Lies, we knew, were the one unforgivable thing – worse, even, than stealing or hitting someone you couldn't stand the sight of any longer.

To lie was to show you didn't believe other people told the truth, either. In the world of the liar, anything goes; and because the liar could get away with it from time to time, the whole thing became doubly dangerous. Elsie's and my teacher, in that long-ago time that was the school summer term we had left behind, with its smell of dusty pavements and May trees in blossom, had told us that Nature never lied – and that we'd be caught out soon enough by Dame Nature herself if we tried it on.

Your nose will grow and grow, our teacher said. Dame Nature doesn't like liars, I can tell you that.

So, as we sat there at Grandmother Dummer's feet, pretending to understand more than we really did (and secretly thinking of Grandmother Dummer as a near relation to Dame Nature, if not that august personage herself), we fingered our noses and wondered if Grandmother Dummer, who is so adept at reading minds, could tell why we suddenly seemed so interested in them.

We knew we'd lied; but it's a shock to hear now that we've been lied to all our lives, as well. How? And, if so, we suddenly don't like the uncertain feeling that grips us in the middle of the tummy and then goes down into our feet and legs.

Some of the lies we've been told, Grandmother Dummer explains, have been good ones. They've been stories – about animals and fairies and trees and flowers that can speak and feel – and they've taught us respect for those other kingdoms where man has gone in and, alas, has wrecked and despoiled without having listened properly to the stories, thinking they're just plain lies.

As it is, said Grandmother Dummer, you've only heard the half of it. And she smiled down at us, as if she wanted to make sure we weren't too disappointed at *Red Riding Hood* – and our favourite, *Cinderella* – being just a pack of lies.

For every fairy story you've had read to you, there's another where the princess is brave and active, and the prince is quiet and likes to play in the long grass by the stream and wait for the little frog to jump out and turn into a strong, beautiful woman in his bed one fine day.

But many of the stories encourage you to see yourselves

as you shouldn't: and that, said Grandmother Dummer, is what I call telling lies.

For instance, do you know why you love that ridiculous flaxen-haired doll with her tinselly clothes and her eyes that are so stupid and so blue? Well, do you?

And Grandmother Dummer told us that we were all – all girls, of course – brought up to believe in the Cinderella story as if it were the gospel truth. (And here, with an embarrassed cough, Grandmother Dummer fell silent for a moment.)

Cinders – there's not a girl in our whole wide world who doesn't wait for her rags to turn to a glittering ball-gown; who doesn't long for that moment – and this is one of the worst lies of all – when she is chosen, singled out.

Who by? By the symbol of power, you nitwits. The prince who will elevate you if you are especially humble, and make you his helpmeet, his very top aide.

Not a girl in the whole wide world who doesn't swallow this lie hook, line and sinker. So why don't women make more things happen for themselves? Ask the tellers of *Cinderella*; ask the stagers of the pantomime, and the crooner of the sugared lies, and the manufacturers of your lovely, brainless dolly.

Ask them and you need look no further, said Grandmother Dummer with a sigh. For what goes in when you're young has the most lasting effect; and there's not a child in kingdom or republic round the world who doesn't secretly know that one day – when they have been sad or lonely, perhaps, or forgotten to bring back the right homework –

the Fairy Godmother will come. And when she comes, it won't be a lie any more. The wish will have come true.

Again, Elsie and I didn't say anything. I'm afraid we did already think that Grandmother Dummer was our Fairy Godmother (as well as being a close relative of Dame Nature, as we said) and we didn't want to admit how many times we'd played coming down in the kitchen in the middle of the night, when the Rayburn stove was out and there was the cold chill of the small hours – and finding the pumpkin we'd smuggled back from an untended garden had turned to a magnificent coach.

As for the ball, we'd taken in turns with our Sindys and Barbies the honour of being picked out by the incredibly handsome, dashing prince.

But after that, somehow, we hadn't known what to do. We weren't sure, even, that we wanted him to come in search of us, with that glass slipper which was agony to wear even if it did fit ...

– Exactly, said Grandmother Dummer, as if she had read our thoughts. The lie of the happy-ever-after. And it goes on today, it swells and multiplies, that powerful, white-icing-ed lie. Why else the bridal magazines, the dream of roses round the door?

– Yes, there is such a thing as happiness, said Grandmother Dummer. But it never comes through lies.

Believe them and you find you're holding a box of chocolates, which, when opened, turn to slugs. A magic box that just disappears when you open it at long last, after all that waiting through the lie for Mr Right.

– So, Grandmother Dummer said, you must know that you'll have to guard against this kind of thing always.

For the horrible fact about little girls who believe the Prince Charming story is that they're specially prepared to stay little girls all their lives.

Rather like stuffing those poor geese in order to make foie gras of their livers. The little girls are kept as little girls, so they're ready to consume the lie, in a variety of different forms – until the day they die.

It suits the advertisers, doesn't it? Little girls who believe a lie, and they become women who believe a lie, will believe all they're told about some lousy product that is there to wash your clothes or get you from A to B.

The makers of lies are the richest people in the land, now. And, however hard little girls struggle to grow up and become people and not just big little girls, the harder the lords of the consumers try to force them to stay for ever in that kitchen waiting for the ball.

– And what was the lie Eve told? Elsie said. We were both shocked, I think, because all the mistakes Eve had made hadn't led us to hate her – quite the opposite, in fact. It was one thing, though, to be a harlot or try to live a crazy life with a congregation, another to tell a lie.

– You must remember, Grandmother Dummer said, that

138

Eve, while apparently to blame for everything that goes wrong in the world, has in fact little choice when it comes to the category in which men place her.

Her circumstances dictate it – or she's been told so many lies when she was a child that she can't tell the truth from fantasy; and she finds herself pigeon-holed once again.

As for friends amongst other women – well, it's very helpful, but very often it's just a palliative – it's easier to moan and then do nothing about it, you see, than to get up and decide on action.

The worst is, too, that many women can't see each other when they're placed in different categories. And that suits our Prince Charming fine.

– It's called, said Grandmother Dummer dreamily – and indeed, she then went on to say it was getting stuffy indoors, with all this talk of lies, and we must all go on the beach for some fresh air – it's called Divide and Rule.

By the time Eve has made her transition, most of those who should be her sisters are strangers to her.

– But, said Grandmother Dummer as we walked along the beach and breathed in the pure air – it smelt of truth, we thought – Eve had to do something, after all.

Eden was a squat when they returned from their travels, and the roof was falling in.

One of the squatters had kept a goat tethered to the old apple tree in the garden – the one, as it happens, that Eve took an apple from, assisted by her friend Frank Blake – and the goat had pulled the tree down and got into the house, where it was munching through all the files of cabinet papers that Adam had been hoping to sell to the press overseas for an enormous sum.

In fact, the goat was just digesting the proof that there had been a cover-up in the water pollution scandal – no, no, I'm not allowed to tell you that, said Grandmother Dummer hastily – when the poor family that the original dwellers in Paradise had been made their appearance there.

The goat hadn't been able to demolish the kitchen table – where the squatters dug into their cans of lifted baked beans and vegetable birianis.

On the last stretch of table available, Eve laid out a cheap lined exercise book and picked up a pen and began to write her lies.

◆

That must have been the night, Elsie and I decided later, when Grandmother Dummer told us about the dreams Eve dreamt – and all for a willing audience, for we dreamt them too, and awoke gasping at the sheer seduction of the web she'd spun for us.

Eden had become a great hospital. We lay entranced in that land half-way between sleep and the recognition of dawn, as nurses bustled, and stretchers on oiled wheels went at a decorous speed down corridors where we could even smell the blend of pine disinfectant and the strong scent of arum lilies from the rooms. (This was a private hospital, Grandmother Dummer told us, and we heard a sorrowful note in her voice. Spinners of romances, like Eve has become, must keep up with the times.)

Eve comes into sight, in our vision of a perfect world, where caps are so brightly starched, and where grieving relatives are given scarcely more than a quarter of a page to themselves; Eve glides rather than walks down the corridor to the operating theatre, while beseeching hands go out to her and she smiles an ineffable smile.

– No, not like her Madonna smile, says Grandmother Dummer. Eve is virgin now, inviolable, in charge of the keys to life and death. Her smile is distant, merciful ... and under her starched cap her hair is red and shiny as a gold coin in the old days years and years before you were born.

– Red hair? asks Elsie. For somehow we had always thought of Eve the temptress as O-blonde (Harlow, Monroe, Bardot, the gorgeous goddesses with a hole in them, as Grandmother Dummer once vulgarly put it, just to show she wasn't stuck in the age of the Brothers Grimm).

– Red hair, we're told firmly. Nurses in the big-selling books have red hair. It's left to the reader to speculate on whether there's fire down below – and with this Grandmother Dummer chuckles and tells us that the business of romance, or the Big Lie as she calls it, is deadly serious.

– It brings in millions, she says. And what could be more serious than that?

– Yes, says Grandmother Dummer, they chop down whole forests for these books, where women can dream their way through the bad parts of life – and the worst of it is that when they wake up things are just as bad if not more terrible than before. They chop down all these trees to make the lies have a home, so that must be serious business, said Grandmother Dummer.

In the hospital is the most advanced brain-transplant unit in the world. The operating room is fixed up like the inside of a spaceship, and the myriad tiny spotlights, which will penetrate the cortex and reveal the secrets of memory, of speech, of precision and imagination, twinkle like a new galaxy overhead.

Few nurses are allowed into the holy of holies, this inner sanctum where Professor Richard Colne can transform at the drop of a hat – if that is the right expression, says Grandmother Dummer amusedly – the kindest of men into a mass murderer, a dribbling idiot into the inventor of quantum theory.

Few nurses, indeed! – but Eve has penetrated deep into this mysterious theatre, where players change on stage as their personalities undergo the delicate attentions of the knife.

And she has penetrated the heart, too, of the incredibly handsome Richard Colne (note that hard C, girls: you will never find a hero in a big lie book with a name like Petty or Sissons).

Mind you, we don't know yet that Richard's lion heart has indeed been touched by Cupid's arrow.

*

We must learn first of the love and longing nursed by nurse Eve for her doctor boss.

How she yearns to get the chance to wash his scalpel!

How many free breaks would she give up to be allowed to snip the catgut that holds the poor patients' wits together!

And, of course, because she works so hard and is so much in love, Eve is finally permitted into the arena of death and rebirth, the operating theatre. She joins the unit! Oh, how happy Eve is now!

◆

What has happened to Adam, and to the children, we want to know. After all, Eve may be happy, but are they getting anything to eat? Who washes Abe and Cain's football shirts, please?

– I see you're well trained already, says Grandmother Dummer with a resigned smile. Adam washes them of course. And he's grateful to do so.

I'll tell you why.

Eve did all she could, at first, to persuade Adam to join in her fantasies. After all, it's grim at Eden, where it rains all the time and the squatters' kids' used bubble-gum sticks to all the furniture, so it's as much as you do to unglue yourself every time you want to get up from a chair.

Eve wants to take Adam out of all that, and make him dream her dream along with her. She wants to make him the brain surgeon of the century, you see.

We said we didn't. How could Adam, who had done no training at all, suddenly find himself in that position, we wanted to know?

– Ah, that's it, sighed Grandmother Dummer. That's the point of fantasy. It's about having something without having to work for it. It's divorced from reality – and that's why it's so popular.

Adam kept his head and settled down to mending the broken tumble-dryer.

Eve by now was head over heels in love with Professor Richard Colne, and he had to put up with her waking in the middle of the night and moaning his name. Once he even woke to find she was scribbling notes on his back.

Poor Adam.

Or so you might say – but surely it's his fault that Eve is in this pickle in the first place. You can hardly be surprised when she weeps and gnashes her teeth at the appearance of a rival – there has to be a rival, of course – who threatens to take away the affections of our glamorous brain-man.

– Oh poor Eve, Elsie and I said, until we remembered that Eve was making all these people up anyway.

– Yes, she modelled the rival on Sally – with a touch of Brigid thrown in, said Grandmother Dummer. They both tried to sue, but they didn't have a leg to stand on.

In our Big Book, the rival must be despatched pretty quickly. And it's when Brigid/Sally tries to barge into the most important brain surgery of the decade, where Professor

Colne is attempting to implant policy-decision-making apparatus into the mind of the President of the United States, that he realizes his terrible mistake in encouraging her and banishes her forever from his team.

Eve reigns alone now, and as – magic moment! – she snips the gut that holds together the brain of the world's most powerful man, she feels Colne's arms, strong and masterful, close around her waist ...

– And then what? say Elsie and I eagerly, for we wonder if Colne has jogged Eve at a crucial moment, or what. Is everything OK?

– Oh, hunky-dory, says Grandmother Dummer. That's the trouble. Richard Colne hates kippers and blows his nose with a sound like an elephant, and snores – and Eve has vaginal thrush – but they're supposed to live happily ever after.

– Well, I ask you! says Grandmother Dummer.

Elsie and I, who had been enjoying the dreams of the hospital over the past nights, must have looked disappointed, because Grandmother Dummer said,

– As long as you don't really believe in these lies, they can be quite harmless. And Eve only believed in them sometimes. At first, that is.

When she wasn't spinning those dreams for Big Little Girls – all of whom become as addicted to them as some kids do to junk food: the Big Book is the monosodium-glutamate of literature – she was a good mother to her children, if rather snappy with Adam because he simply didn't measure up to her idea of a Romantic Hero.

Eden looks better, too, because as the money comes in the squatters are bought flats by Eve and she can afford to have the carpet cleaned. Even the damp and cracked front porch gets a going-over.

You'd think Eve would stop now. After all, she's made quite a bit. They've had a holiday in Disneyland and there's a new Aga, which Adam stokes with solid fuel to give a country atmosphere to their new oak and Provençal-blind kitchen. Life is pretty comfortable for the first nuclear family.

The trouble is, Eve can't stop. She's as addicted as her readers, and as their pathetic pleas for more come through the post, she begins to feel as starved of a 'fix' as they evidently do.

We all know, said Grandmother Dummer, that Satan doesn't so much find work for idle hands as make hands that are already leading the world astray go even faster and for greater profit.

And so you can't say you're surprised when I tell you that Eve received a phone-call from the most powerful publisher of Big Lies in international book-production. He would like Eve to come to his skyscraper office, he would like to buy her lunch.

And before you could say 'no orchids for Miss Blandish', there is Eve, with a corsage flown in fresh from the Sultan of

Brunei, discussing her contract over lunch with none other than our old friend, Frank Blake.

◆

– Mind you, said Grandmother Dummer, as Elsie and I recoiled at being reminded of that evil man – mind you, Eve and the Serpent *did* have a partnership back in the days of Eden, as you remember. And you can't tell me she didn't see something of the Devil in Professor Richard Colne, the brain surgeon who took her heart and then made an honest woman of her, in the face of stiff competition. If he was her meal ticket for life, then she was his meal. There's always something of the rabbit and the snake in these romances, ended Grandmother Dummer thoughtfully.

However that may be, Eve was too dumb at first to see that Frank Blake was an adept at disguise.

To take her out to lunch at the Carlton Towers he appeared as Groucho Marx, complete with cigar and carnation in his buttonhole, and a bucket of champagne in which he'd stuck a single red rose that kept falling out and drenching them both with water.

Oh, he was a cunning one, the emissary of Satan. He was so touchingly, bunglingly inept that he won Eve's heart straight away – if he'd been a smooth Hollywood producer, after all, she might well have decided she was satisfied with what she had got, and gone home to Adam and the boys, chucking out the microwave and the freezer on arrival.

As it was, Eve thought little harm could come from Frank Blake's suggestion.

– You'll find a first-class ticket in your napkin, Blake chortled; and they both burst out laughing again when a Pullman first-class single dropped straight from the monogrammed linen into the bouillabaisse à la Cap d'Antibes Picasso.

– It will be your greatest success yet, purred Frank Blake, as he wiped off the garlic *rouille* and surreptitiously phoned, from a cellular appendage under the table, to the station to lay on a private train.

– You'll see the kind of world you are about to enter, hissed Blake as they walked the length of red carpet on the platform, and he handed Eve into her private drawing-room on wheels.

– The trains always stopped for the Lacey family on the outskirts of the estate, my dear Eve. And now – in anticipation of your visit – they will do so again.

– So, Grandmother Dummer said, Eve finds herself on a train all to herself, going north. Home and children seem miles away as she looks forward to the saga for which Frank Blake has given her such an enormous advance – and in dollars too! As I said, children, Eve isn't entirely innocent of what she's doing.

She knows as well as anyone else that she has become a courtesan.

– In the old days, Grandmother Dummer said, a courtesan was something you could hardly pin down – except, of course, that that's exactly what they were – pinned down, I mean. But to describe them in any way as a harlot would be quite inaccurate.

You see, for one thing the harlot simply doesn't know who her customer is. (Look at Eve, anonymous to Adam, and she didn't know him from himself.)

Whereas the courtesan makes it her business to know every single thing about her client – or patron, or benefactor, or however she might like to call the guy who picks up the tab.

A good courtesan knows precisely the vintage of the claret from the tiny vineyard, where once his grandmother took him as a child and he felt on his palate for the first time the heavenly sensation of the fermented grape.

She knows his sock size at Turnbull and Asser; and why he likes steak and kidney pudding without the kidney.

She knows his favourite fairy tale is *Mother Goose* and his favourite songs are all from *Showboat*.

– Does that sound old-fashioned to you? You're dead right it does, said Grandmother Dummer when we signalled our incomprehension of such a person as the courtesan being able to survive in that way today.

Of course she couldn't: there are too many round-the-world jetters for any one zillionaire to have a single mistress waiting to pin a bunch of Sweet William in his buttonhole every time he comes back from a trip.

And the courtesans have adapted accordingly. Eve, as so many of her sisters, is owned now not by a French Baron or Northern industrialist but by a mega-corporation, such as the one headed by Frank Blake, which has eyes all over space and satellite dishes to catch their tears in the gardens of the bored and sad.

Eve is the slave of multimedia millions; and having graduated with her doctor-nurse schlockerations, she must now proceed to the estate of the Earls of de Lacey. Oh yes, she must, girls, for she has taken the Devil's handout, said Grandmother Dummer, when we looked apprehensive at this.

Frank Blake, you see, likes to disguise himself as the Romantic Hero – isn't it strange there's inevitably something 'Satanic' about the hero, as if what the Serpent knew all along were really true, that women love a touch of evil, to cheer up their monotonous lives – and Frank Blake, who has mysteriously got to the estate of the de Laceys before Eve's private train, is there to meet her on the little rustic platform.

Of course, Eve doesn't recognize him. I mean, when Frank Blake was the bumbling pin-striped publisher in the Carlton Towers it would have seemed impossible that he could have transformed himself into Anthony de Lacey, fifteenth Earl and seventieth Viscount of Rushdie in Co. Clare, Knight of the Wright's Templars.

And so it never crossed Eve's mind, as she was handed down from her private carriage – converted from a sleeper of Queen Victoria's daughter Princess Adelaide, and richly hung with the skins of tigers shot by Earl de Lacey's grandfather on safari in India on the eve of Independence – that the incredibly handsome man who strode forth from under a canopy hung with little baskets of country flowers, and invited her to come up to the house in his pony and trap, was in fact none other than Old Nick himself.

– To complicate matters further, said Grandmother Dummer, Eve's lordling was in fact descended from the Devil. (You remember Cruella surely?) His lip curled – yes, I'm afraid Satanically, said Grandmother Dummer, laughing. And his lean, hungry face had a scar from a duel fought in his youth over the favours of Lady Clare de Vere de Vere. (He won, natch; but Lady Clare died, as so many heroines must, of some wasting disease or another.) And that leaves the field absolutely clear for Eve.

A field, I may say, is what the de Lacey estate is not. Vastmere, for that is the name of the hundred thousand acres or so owned since time immemorial by the de Laceys, has parks and parterres and staircases of moving water, and greenhouses so big and choked with palms and hanging jungle creepers that you could keep an elephant in one – and indeed Anthony (as we shall daringly call him) does. (If Eve is reminded for one sickening moment of the brothel where Frank Blake made her climb astride a Manchester businessman and sit perched there in a howdah, she says nothing.)

For, after all, Frank Blake took all her earnings in her Mayfair days. And now he will allow Eve ten per cent of the revenue of the sales of the Vastmere Trilogy. And a percentage of the film money too! Eve knows when she's lucky, I can tell you.

*

151

The trouble is, how to get started.

And it seems, for the first time in her writing life, that Eve has a writer's block.

Maybe it's something to do with the awesomeness of the lineage of de Lacey (for many are still very impressed in England, and in America too, by the ways of the old aristocracy; and if they weren't, Frank Blake wouldn't pay Eve so much to write a romance about them).

Or maybe it's the lord's habit of keeping a hooded falcon on his wrist just at the most intimate moments and removing the hood at the very instant when his hot, hard and passionate lips are about to meet Eve's, in a Georgian Temple of Love in the park by the ha-ha.

Eve has had many a bodice ripped by the talons of that vicious falcon.

Not surprisingly, she finds it hard to open her laser-writer, which will beam her lies on wealth and handsome earls and happy-ever-after to Frank Blake's office hundreds of miles away.

And as each day passes, the silence becomes more oppressive and the receptor machine in Frank Blake's office lies idle.

– As you can imagine, children, Eve's proprietor and publisher is feeling a lot more frustrated than he allows himself to let on.

After all, if Mr Ten-Dollars-a-Word rapes the silly woman, fifty million readers are gone at a stroke. For, apart from some heavy breathing and a scene where Eve is found in the bath in the de Lacey rubies, given her at the moment of her sweet, yielding acceptance of Anthony de Lacey's proposal of marriage, there has been no hard sex at all.

Frank Blake knows he must not kill the goose who has been paid in gold to lay the golden egg.

But several times he can hardly control himself; and there is a nasty accident on a pheasant shoot followed by an overturned Land-Rover from which Eve miraculously escapes.

– No – and here Grandmother Dummer looked sad again – Eve only broke her block when she realized she had begun to believe entirely in her creation.

In love with the last of the de Laceys, and about to bear his child, Eve sat down in her boudoir in Castle Rushdie one fine morning and began to write.

She knew, as she did so, that she would never go back to Adam again.

– I suppose, said Grandmother Dummer, when we had contemplated Eve alone in the palatial halls of Vastmere, with the wind whistling on the moors outside and the wicked, hawk-nosed earl, a cross between Mr Rochester and Heathcliff with a touch of Humphrey Bogart in *Casablanca* thrown in, striding into her bedchamber and taking her, lifeless with desire, in his arms ...

– I suppose you could say that Eve sold her soul to the Devil, Grandmother Dummer said. For the Vastmere Trilogy made her vastly rich, you know. She could afford to buy Adam a stud; and a yacht, a three-masted schooner which sailed round the world with its great black and gold sails like some gigantic moth of an Oriental night. She could – and did – set Cain up in a martial arts academy of his own, where he could practise killing to his heart's content. Abe she sent to agricultural college before presenting him with a farm half the size of Wales.

But Adam wasn't happy with the way things were. Oh good God no.

– So why doesn't she go back to him? said Elsie, although we both somehow knew the answer. Eve was in love with a man of her dreams – literally. How could Adam compare with this paper lover?

– It's not just that, said Grandmother Dummer. Eve can't go back to Adam because the balance of power between them has changed for good.

Adam could love her when he was on top. And we've seen what happens to him when he isn't.

He could be her child, her master, her pimp. But – not yet, anyway – he can't be simply her inferior.

Inferior in every way, mind you. Less handsome than Earl de Lacey, for whom five hundred million women swoon from Singapore to Dunedin.

Less rich – by far. What can Adam give a woman who has everything for her birthday?

So, for a while, he stays quietly in Eden, which is photographed frequently for the glossy magazines these days, as the home of the prolific and internationally acclaimed merchant of desire, Eve (although she seldom bothers to be in the pictures, and we see Adam and Seth, hair brushed neatly and white collars and grey suits, standing by the baronial fireplace and looking as if they're just waiting for their dear one to come in).

Then, he files for divorce.

Adam has become a bitter person. Despite the big allowance Eve sends him from Vastmere, he wants more. No one recognizes *him* in the street and he wants compensation.

And he has no hobbies, nothing to distract him from this terrible envy and hatred of Eve. For women, you see, are not supposed to be more successful than men, and must try to conceal it if they are, instead of flaunting it, which I'm afraid Eve has rather taken to doing.

The divorce papers arrive at Vastmere and Eve frowns in displeasure.

The King and Queen of Morocco were due to visit Eden next weekend and she was counting on Adam to look after the entertaining side of it, while she helicoptered down late on the Friday night after a continuation of the saga, where Lord de Lacey finds an illegitimate peasant half-sister in his Irish estates and brings her home to meet his wife.

How can Eve possibly deliver in time if there is no one to act as housekeeper in Eden?

But Adam is adamant. No house-husband he. And he wants fifty per cent of her royalties for life.

Now Eve has to sell out even further. (And I may tell you, children, that when I said earlier I thought she had sold her soul to the Devil, it wasn't by accident that I sounded slightly doubtful. For it's doubtful in itself, if you look back over history, whether the idea of a woman having a soul was ever taken very seriously. Certainly, a woman's soul never carried the same weight as a man's; and I don't think Satan, or his emissary Mephistopheles Blake, took the trouble to go around offering pacts for them, they were worth so little.)

All the same, Eve knows she's worth a good deal to Frank Blake Enterprises Ltd. And she finds herself in a double bind – for just as she can't stop loving Lord de Lacey, and as she wants to go on getting richer and richer, so Adam wants more and more as well. They're like the fairy story of the old woman who lived in a vinegar bottle and was granted three wishes – she wished first for a house and then for a mansion and then for a palace, and, finally, to be Pope. You can guess where she ended – right back in the raspberry vinegar, of course.

The trouble is, Adam wants his share of that vinegar bottle, too. He's experiencing for the first time all the anger and frustration of an abandoned wife; and if he hears Lilith laughing her head off on stormy nights while he hangs about the gates of Vastmere (he can't get in because private guards and electronic surveillance make Castle Rushdie impregnable) he is determined not to let his resolve weaken.

Half of everything! And that includes the de Laceys' valuable property holdings in London's Kensington.

Eve meets Frank Blake in the Savoy. She's pale and harassed, and not for the first time Frank Blake considers taking a contract out on Adam, so that Eve can fulfil the terms of hers with Mega Lies in peace.

When he hears, however, what Eve proposes to do for F. B. Enterprises Ltd he comes to the conclusion that the death of Adam might be too much of a distraction for the projected Biggest Lie of them All – and he knows, too, that if you slay Adam another one springs up in his place, as you can't have a world without men.

So, over his Tequila Tropical Sunset, Frank looks innocently pleased to hear that Eve has completed *Blackthorn Winter*, where Lord de Lacey's wicked stepmother tries to seduce him while Eve is bearing their heir, and asks what next she has in mind for him.

(He has a good idea, of course. Because the Devil likes to keep women in their rightful place; and lately there's just been too much chatting about rebellion and escape. A meeting at top level has recently decided a more cunning way than usual to deal with this insurrection must be found.)

And who better to lead the new reaction – and disguised while doing so as an archangel of feminism, a herald of free opportunity and equity – than Eve?

True, she has a reputation for fuelling the dreams of women who know no better with her tales of wanton maids and darkling landowners or brain surgeons. But there's nothing easier for a woman than to repent, and to announce that she has seen the light.

The profits from *Balloons of Vertigo*, the Serpent calculated, would be triple all Eve's earnings from her other works.

For, by taking the story of a woman who battles through to success and self-awareness in a male-dominated world – by portraying this theme with a veneer of reality, while in reality writing a fairy tale just as pernicious as the rest – Eve can be assured of truly global film tie-in interest and royalties from all those dupes who think it's as easy as Eve makes out to be a woman and go it alone.

– Not, said Grandmother Dummer, that it's not possible to point to successful women – and to see that there are more of them, perhaps, than there were.

But Eve, with her lies, forgets the anguish she suffered herself. She forgets the nappies; and the pain of Adam's lack of love for her when Cain and Abe were born; and the way she had to do things she didn't want, just in order to keep alive.

She forgets the sneers of the world – or, if she wishes to show them she makes the scene glamorous somehow, set in the Colony Room or le Gavroche, where a rich man, after putting down the heroine, suddenly is seen to fancy her too.

So what's new, I ask you?

It's all a sleight of hand, lying. And Eve has become supremely good at it.

Frank Blake sends her to a ranch on the West Coast of Australia so that she can write in absolute peace and quiet. He sees that Adam is paid off handsomely in the divorce;

and he thinks he's seen the last of him (Frank Blake's first stupid mistake).

Lilith takes Cain and Abe to the South of France on holiday; and to show her contempt for Eve's lies she blows the top off the casino at Monte Carlo and scatters banknotes and gold plaques right into the streets and over the sea wall into the sea.

There's only one way to show the world what you mean, says Lilith as she's carted off to prison. But she gets out, naturally, by making such a violent *mistral* that prisoners long ago locked up for a *crime passionel* awake and dream of doing it all over again – and in the ensuing riot Lilith rejoins her stepsons at St Paul de Vence.

– Oh dear, where was I? said Grandmother Dummer, for she had noticed it was getting late. (Indeed, the grandfather clock had chimed nine times; and although we were easily old enough now to know that the grandfather clock didn't, as we used to think when we were very small, really have Grandfather Dummer concealed inside it, we were a little frightened as always to hear those solemn notes.)

– Eve's book sold one hundred million copies, said Grandmother Dummer. And Eve moved permanently to the Connaught Hotel.

– And there, my dears, said Grandmother Dummer, there's the rub.

◆

The summer was coming to a close. Grandmother Dummer had taken us to the Tinner's Arms – so low-beamed and murky you could well believe in pirates and smugglers – and even in the strange tale one man spun of a returning sailor and the woman who was barmaid and recognized him for the man who got her with child all of sixteen years ago.

And the man who wrote that story, said Grandmother Dummer, came to live here – not at Zennor but five miles up the coast at Tregarthen, and his name was Lawrence.

– He was a famous writer, Grandmother Dummer said. And the most famous of his books is called *Women in Love*.

Elsie and I wanted to run out on to the steep grass by the Tinner's Arms and then down the lanes, bordered with fuchsias still and buzzing with small wasps, to the edge of the cliff. There was a cove you could scramble down to from there; and even Grandmother Dummer with her undoubted magical powers wouldn't be able to follow us there.

We felt sad for Eve, I suppose; for it seemed that by gaining so much fame and fortune, she had lost everything; and we couldn't help wondering if Seth was lonely without her and if Adam's socks needed mending. (Children are such conservatives, as Grandmother Dummer used to say to us with a fond smile, as if she didn't realize that we'd already decided somehow to combine earning money and an interesting career with rows of little bootees on the line.)

But …

*

160

– There's the rub, Grandmother Dummer was saying in a sad sort of voice, and we couldn't leave her.

Because Eve was on her own now and immensely success-ful, she started to dream of falling in love. (I think she may have read *Women in Love* when she was a girl, you know; but what life had actually been like was far from Lawrence's fantasies of sexual partnership – although he probably got the male predominance part right.)

No, Eve has time now and to spare. She feels that if she looks really hard she'll find the perfect man: the new man, if you like.

And Grandmother Dummer laughed and her laugh turned into a cough and we had to fetch her a pint of porter from the old oak bar.

– You see, said Grandmother Dummer when she had drunk her fill, Eve felt that she'd been poor and in thrall to Adam when they first met. Eden had been his, after all, and the shock of finding out about Lilith and the subsequent divorce had made everything really hard for her.

Even when Adam was poor, too, as we have seen, it didn't help bring a sense of equality to their marriage.

So surely, now that Eve is rich – rich beyond the wildest dreams of any of God's creatures, whether shameful man in his fallen Paradise, or mammon beast in his tower of dollars and yen – now must be the time to redress the balance.

After all, Eve is quite happy to make a generous settle-ment on the man who makes her happy.

And that man can run a few businesses for her, too, to

keep him busy while she writes of further adventures in the life of the mega-successful heroine of *Balloons of Vertigo*, Holly Spine.

For the right man, Eve has in mind a yacht and a private Concorde and as much Neapolitan ice-cream as he wants flown in every day in a great refrigerated cone.

The trouble is, as Eve discovers, a good man is hard to find.

And especially if you're rich and successful.

What is it about those publishing parties Frank Blake throws for her in the Connaught Hotel – those book launches on a cruiser on the Thames – that make men turn away from Eve as if she had grown old and ugly?

A crowd of women surge up for a signed copy of Holly's latest vicissitudes and triumphs in the face of male resistance (in the latest volume Holly is an underwater diver who stumbles on a cache of gold from the Spanish Armada and has to fight off male predators from all over the world in order to claim her rightful treasure) – but no men want even a signal from those eyes once so desirable and smouldering.

Oh my God, says Eve. I *am* getting old and ugly. Oh my God, what am I going to do?

– Now, as you must have seen, children, Eve is getting more and more entangled in her own lies. Her heroine Holly Spine hasn't worn make-up for years – and was seen throwing her lipstick over Brooklyn Bridge, in the first of the sagas. (She guardedly took some attention to her face when power dressing came in, and Joan Collins's shoulder pads needed to be written into the script.)

But the point about Holly as a whole is that she is immune to the power of her own femininity – indeed, being a black belt at judo, she soon despatches any man who dares to presume that 'your place or mine?' means anything more than a choice of offices for signing the latest deal.

– So what do you do when you don't need the black belt judo any more? said Grandmother Dummer. And we could see she was smiling, at last, as if the ludicrousness of Eve's situation was beginning to come home to her. After all, Eve sent monthly cheques of a quite staggering size to Adam and Seth; and the other two boys were provided for. Eve herself was safe and sound financially for the rest of her life – so why worry about something silly like no one coming up to you at a party and making a pass?

– But she did, said Grandmother Dummer.

Eve tried everything. She had her face remodelled entirely, and her hair dipped in honey gathered from the bees of Mount Athos, where no woman has ever been seen. She had a new outline to her body drawn by Christian Lacroix; and the requisite surgery to make herself that outline – which was somewhere, said Grandmother Dummer, laughing again, between a mermaid and Playmate of the Month.

She had boudoir photos taken – by a woman photographer, of course – of Eve in white satin cami-knickers, Eve naked except for a swansdown boa, Eve in a black suspender belt and nothing else.

The photos were distributed and sales soared (for, in this age of contradictions, no one minded the fact that this great feminist writer was also posing like a Page Three model. It just showed how up-to-date she was).

But no man appeared to escort Eve to the romantic dinners of which she dreamed.

At balls she danced with the presidents of the biggest media corporations, who were so anxious to keep her in their stable they hardly dared let a hand alight on her restructured, snowy shoulder.

Bouquets arrived every day – but they were anonymous, from Hollywood or sometimes from a Women's Institute in the depths of the provinces, the members writing ecstatically, on the accompanying card, that Holly Spine had liberated them from their lives as doormat wives and they were leaving home to find freedom and adventure.

Good luck to you, Eve said under her breath each time one of these tributes appeared.

For to be liberated, as she has discovered, is to be free for no one at all. Especially, of course, if you are a woman and successful.

A real man, as Eve sadly decided, is put off by that.

– It is time, said Grandmother Dummer, to draw a veil over Eve's behaviour at this point.

I can only imagine that lies breed lies – and Eve is desperately lonely by now and will do anything to get Adam back. (Adam had married a nice, quiet, dark girl and they'd settled in the country, on the allowed percentage of Eve's royalties – which comes to quite a bit, of course – in a cottage with roses and honeysuckle round the door.)

– Ouch! said Grandmother Dummer. Eve really minds that. She takes Seth out, in his rare exeats from the expensive public school where he was sent when Eve began to write – but Seth, although polite to his mother, does seem a good deal more interested in cricket and football; and in the possibility of a fishing holiday with his father and his nice new stepmother Lucy in the north of Scotland in the summer holidays.

Poor Eve. Her about-turn was just as successful as the position she had held before.

For Holly Spine suddenly, in *A Child to Remember*, becomes the biggest anti-abortionist you ever knew in your life. She marches in defiance of the cruel murder of unborn children. She proclaims the happiness of Muslim women; and she exalts the virtues of arranged marriages in general, preferably with a birth-control-free litter of children. Informed that Islam will not take her because of her brazen past, Holly joins the Roman Catholic Church.

– And so, and here Grandmother Dummer stood up and strode out of the Tinner's Arms so we had to run, after all, to get out there just ahead of her.

– So, said Grandmother Dummer, did Eve. The Pope writes her a letter of congratulation. Frank Blake, furious at first, tots up the number of Catholics in underdeveloped

countries and calls for mass translation into Spanish and
Portuguese.

Eve doesn't know if she's on her head or her heels. Until
she meets Sally again, that is.

◆

– There comes a time in women's lives, said Grandmother
Dummer, when it's just more fun to do things with another
woman – anyway, Eve had enjoyed herself a lot with Sally
before, if you remember, when they dressed up and walked
across London as Jacques and his master.

In those days, though, Eve still had hopes that she would
meet up with Adam again – or with someone very like him,
at least.

Now she's not so sure. It seems the whole world is out
there waiting to be saved by her; and the trouble is that
Sally, who has reached much the same conclusion, is only
too eager to aid and abet her old friend the new billionairess,
creator of Holly Spine.

Holly, with all her sufferings and her change of character
and opinion at just the time when public opinion is moving
firmly into the post-Aids era of moral severity and conserva-
tive taste, has so vast a readership that any movement
spearheaded by her creator is bound to attract an instant and
global audience.

So Eve founds the Green Chastity Party.
At first, as she and Sally go out in search of recruits, quite

a few mistakes are made. Eve listens to a battered wife and goes out to find the husband, Sally in tow and horse-whip at the ready.

Oh dear! Eve is just so naive! Even Sally blenches when she offers the battering brute thousands to keep away from his wife – only to find, after he has pocketed the cheque, that this was a part of a wicked little consortium that goes around preying on the generosity of liberals such as Eve, with all her embarrassing wealth. Bruises and scars washed off, Luigi's moll is holidaying happily with him now in Majorca.

The same is true when Eve gives as her aim for the Green Chastity Party the abolition of the Right in Britain and the United States of America.

So many students and nurses and teachers and young unemployed join – all the miserable beggars, too, are given free membership by Eve and Sally – but as most of the members of the party have nowhere to live and have therefore not registered to vote, the parties of Reaction go on just as before, when all is said and done.

Eve and Sally, our brave Donna Quixote and Sancha Panza, tilt at many such windmills, I fear.

They're up against the real world, you see, and they can't see it.

And Eve has lived in a web of fabrications; of romance; of sheer unmitigated lies for as long as she can remember.

It's time to change.

And if it hadn't been for the launch party for the positively last Holly Spine book – in which the heroine throws her cap to the winds and becomes pregnant with sextuplets

– our brave adventurers would doubtless have gone off in Eve's rose-coloured yacht *Rosinante*, to cruise the Seychelles before they subside altogether with the raising of the watermark worldwide and the warming of the atmosphere.

– You see, said Grandmother Dummer, already Eve's next incarnation has begun to weigh heavily on her.

But for the time being, at the party in the Oliver Messel suite at the Dorchester, where the waiters are circulating with caviar cakes made in the shape of Holly's pussy and stuffed with glacé cherries, all she can see is the bronzed, lean man who walks towards her and then stops with a provocative smile playing on his lips – just like the hero in all of Eve's books.

– Don't ask me why Eve hadn't learnt her lesson by now, Grandmother Dummer said with a noisy sigh. (By this time we were standing on the cliff's edge and staring out to sea. Already, the fading summer could be seen in the light on the intense blue, going from mauve to a deep purple – and we could have sworn we saw Eve floating there in a bath of her favourite colour, clad in wisps of the sea and splashing away out of sight like a mermaid.)

But she wanted to be young just a little longer, I suppose.

Because it was Adam standing there, of course.

Don't ask me if he left the quiet, dark Lucy because he couldn't stand their pig-tailed daughters and the pony club and sailing off the coast of Suffolk when there was time for a holiday break.

Don't ask me if he thought of Eve's billions with greed, and felt he'd like to get his hands on them.

After all, toyboys – and this is what Adam had become – are expected to profit from their associations with rich and powerful women: just as much as Pamella Bordes with all those cabinet ministers and royalty and with a good deal less hypocrisy from the tabloid press.

Anyone taking one look at Adam could tell he was just made for Eve.

Their eyes met – and melted.

They kissed; and everyone at the party applauded, and bottles of strawberry-pink champagne from the cellars of Louis XVI at Fontainebleau were opened with a series of pops like fireworks going off.

From the roof of the Dorchester a splendid firework display did now take place. Holly's body, splendidly adorned with rockets that shot from the tits and a Catherine wheel that kept the pelvis in constant motion, like a gorgeous belly-dancer of the galaxy, danced in the darkening skies for the benefit of Frank Blake Enterprises.

Georgian vodka, each priceless bottle with its blade of bison grass from the entrance to the cave where the centenarians guard their secret of eternal life, was cracked open with the blade of Pushkin's sword and drunk down by the excited guests.

Oblivious to all this, Eve and Adam lay under the canopy in the Harlequin Room, where the colours from the motley velvets and silks made a jest of their frenzied passion.

(As for Sally, Eve was to agree on a share of Adam, after the first ecstatic chapter of their romance. Toyboys, like callgirls, are hardly exclusive property.)

– I'm shocking you again, said Grandmother Dummer, for she must have seen us look sad at the mercenary nature of Eve's relations with Adam.

But, quite honestly, a rich and successful woman, as we have seen, is considered to have been de-sexed by her achievements and wealth.

The first Queen Elizabeth had to keep all her courtiers in control; and was careful as to how she dispensed her favours.

So must Eve be careful; and she's grateful for Sally, their quixotic period being over and their crusade to save the world having done little more than make Eve, paradoxically, richer – for the more she gave away to poor countries, the more her grateful banks, cancelling the international debt, were prepared to lend her for investment in industry.

(Ah yes. Eve lied again, and she knew it. She was Green. And yet her money went through the hands of her stockbrokers to the mines of South Africa, to the aluminium-dense water plants in countries excessively affected by drought; to research on poor and innocent animals for the sake of the development of a drug to save the only vile dweller on the planet, man.)

However hard she tried, Eve took away with one hand what she gave with the other. This was capitalism, and her lies had made her lie on a world scale.

*

– So, as Sally murmured while they sat in the sunset on their terrace in the Parioli district of Rome and sipped Negroni and ate little squares of *croûton* with black olives and a sliver of goat's cheese – why not fiddle while it all burns? Yet ...

Adam, lying on a chaise-longue on the ceramic floor of the lofty, vaulted drawing-room, yawns while Eve and Sally examine their consciences amidst all this comfort and splendour.

He consults his watch – the latest model by the world's most precise and exquisite clockmaker, which can calculate leap centuries every four hundred years and permutate annually the date of Easter – and suggests a mouthful down at the Piazza Navona, where all the film-makers go (some of them hoping to get their next project financed by Eve and her empire).

Adam had been to the Maldives and has acquired a deeper tan, his eyes are sapphire-blue above an Armani light summer suit that is the colour of a bleached wheatfield – like his hair, smoothly combed back in the faintly ridiculous but endearing Mafia look that proclaims him every inch a disguised English gentleman.

He has ski'd this year already at Klosters and spent a couple of weeks in Manhattan in their apartment at the very summit of the Waldorf Towers, where the wind whistles so hard in the elevator that he is occasionally unpleasantly reminded of his poor days in the room with the crack in the ceiling in the communal dump he and Eve had to share when they were thrown out of Eden.

Adam has been skin-diving in Petit St Vincent, and driven his racing car, especially designed to a secret recipe for success by the partner of Donald Campbell, and he has watched his bay mare Evedrops win the Grand National without any difficulty at all – while the Queen of England wept with disappointment in the Royal Box.

Poor Adam! No wonder he's getting bored. Eve is grating on his nerves – and neither she nor Sally, for all the cosmetic surgery in the world, is exactly a spring chicken. All this talk of the future of the world tires him exceedingly; and he comes out on the magnificent terrace, with its mosaic of jade and lapis-lazuli, and looks pointedly at his watch again, this watch that will be able to tell him, in four hundred years' time, when it's a leap century and he might find himself receiving a proposal of marriage from a lovely young maiden.

Somehow the watch and its foolish predictions are too much for Eve.

She rises to her feet, goes over to him and pulls the intricate, million-dollar precision device from his wrist; the bracelet holding it (of silver studded with tiny diamonds that spell A-D-A-M) snaps and falls to the terrace floor: the time machine, tossed by Eve high out into the street, sails briefly in the evening breeze and then falls, dashed to smithereens, in a small private park beside a fountain with a stone basin and a marble nymph.

Adam jumps toward the parapet – then, mindful as ever of his safety and the need to preserve his beauty in the precarious profession he has taken up, draws back.

Eve stares at him with contempt. For the first time, as if the marble nymph hundreds of feet below in the dusty little park were speaking, and not herself, Eve speaks the truth.

From the mouths of babes, they say ...

... and for a short flicker of time Adam thinks he sees that nymph pout her stone lips and a gush of old Apuleian wine issue forth from them. *In vino veritas*, you might say.

But whatever the reason, Eve is undergoing the distinctly unaccustomed sensation of speaking the truth.

THERE IS NO TIME BUT THIS TIME TO SAVE THE PLANET FROM EXTINCTION, Eve says.

And at that moment Eve stopped being a courtesan, and Frank Blake's shares crashed on Wall Street; and Lilith sent a great thunderstorm, which filled the Colosseum with hailstones the size of big cats and tigers.

While Adam, still foolishly determined to save his priceless timepiece from destruction, went over to the private escalator, pressed the button and went down.

BLUESTOCKING

You might imagine, Grandmother Dummer said, that Eve's life would be infinitely improved once she became established as a famous scientist.

At first, it was true, to find she could develop her brain – and it wasn't just science she took up: her invitations for sherry at the eminent college of which she was Emeritus Professor were unfailingly issued in Linear B, the language of the Minoans – was intoxicating enough.

Yes, Adam came too; and from the very first this was far from successful: even when he trained himself and became a solid state chemist he was still miles behind Eve in sheer intelligence and application, and he didn't like that one bit, as you don't need telling.

– You can see the way Adam dislikes Eve's cleverness and status as a physicist and leading molecular biologist by the way he reacts, I suppose, Grandmother Dummer said when we pressed her for examples of Adam's less than generous approach to Eve's genius. (Surely Adam ought to be grateful, we argued, to be with a woman as brilliant as any he was likely to meet: isn't it more exciting, more *fun*, simply, to be with a woman of superior intelligence than with a dumb blonde or a nincompoop?)

– Well no, said Grandmother Dummer. That's the distinctly strange part. Women have actually had to pretend they were stupid, to get by – and, if you remember, Eve has decided to give up telling Lies for ever.

It doesn't take her long, as you can imagine, to discover exactly what her options are, in this world of extreme academic brilliance; and it doesn't take her long, either, to see that a woman with even the most modest talents is pushed out and driven into silence. Or, added Grandmother Dummer with a sigh, into the madhouse, or the gas oven (in the old days, that is: suicide can be more easily planned these days, just send your gifted woman writer or painter to live near a nuclear energy station or near one of the polluted rivers of our despoiled planet and she hasn't a chance of surviving and developing her promise).

– No, seriously, said Grandmother Dummer (though we thought she was being quite serious enough) – just consider the great artists, like Rodin, with his beautifully expressive – in bronze, of course – mistress Camille Claudel, who spends her last thirty years locked away in an asylum, 'mad', according to her relatives – but mad in that very sensible American use of the word, just plain angry at the terrible way the great man treated her and the world treated her work.

Think of Alice James, sister of the prolific, long-winded, bearded Henry; the turn of the screw came for her with breast cancer and the possibility of using her own mind – for she was formidably clever and imaginative – taken from her by the women's disease.

We've been looking at those fairy-tale pictures by Kandinsky – my dears, his wife was a superior painter by far: her name was Gabriella Munthe, and she forfeited her entire career for Vassily.

Tell me – and here Grandmother Dummer looked severely at Elsie, who had only this morning cried out that the strange shapes of driftwood and the rotting hull of a boat 'were just like the picture indoors at the house in Zennor' – tell me if you think that the Surrealist painting you admire is by a woman or a man. Ha! – as poor Elsie, who had thought it by a man, blushes and looks to me for reassurance – I can tell you it is by a woman, Leonora Carrington; and that she, like the other women in the Surrealist movement who happened to be women, was considered a good subject, a perfect Muse for a male painter, but definitely not to be encouraged to daub herself.

Yes, we know different now, but we are only just beginning. How long did it take the wounded, extraordinary images of Frieda Kahlo to break loose from the prison of their creator's gender? While her lover Diego Rivera went on to become Mexico's – and Latin America's – most famous artist? Too long, children, too many years after her tortured death.

But it doesn't take long for Eve to see that the very presence of Adam (plotting as he undoubtedly is to outdo her with his cure for cancer, his miracle drug for transsexuals, which will turn a man into a woman overnight and back again, in case of changes of mind and all the other drawbacks that flesh is heir to; and his astounding reversal of Aids into a mild case of acne) – that the presence of Adam in her life, as I say, is dangerous in the extreme. One look at history tells that women who succeed in intellectual pursuits or artistic careers are single, celibate, childless, Gwen John and certainly not Augustus. Just try and envisage the woman don – or painter – with a man in every port and a bun in the oven. We know where that leads – Eve has done with being the single parent who must rise at 5 a.m. if she is to read even the simplest of tracts. So – yes, there is no solution here other than this – Eve must once again find Sally.

Look at Virginia Woolf, girls, and her escapades with Vita Sackville-West, her resulting fantasy of Orlando, the androgynous, transhistorical heroine. (Adam is definitely not working on a miracle drug for women to become men; he's aggrieved enough already at the 'male domain' of the intelligence having been appropriated by his wife.)

Dream tonight of the Ladies of Llangollen, those eminently well-brought-up young damsels of the eighteenth century who ran away together to the hills of Wales, to lie in each others' arms and talk of poetry …

Well, why not, said Grandmother Dummer, as she saw Elsie look at me and then away at the ground – and then my own eyes wandering, dreaming, as if some seed of love were already there between us. Why not? Are we put into this world only and exclusively to find a partner of the male sex?

Mind you, said Grandmother Dummer, Eve's marriage to

Sally wasn't entirely successful. I have to say that the idea wasn't new, either: in the century even before those young women of Llangollen, who invited the daughter of the King of France's brother to listen to their Aeolian harp, played nightly by the wind; and entertained the great men of the time – Coleridge and Southey and Wordsworth all travelling from far away to witness the miracle of two clever women in love and living together in harmony – one hundred years before, I may tell you, a brilliantly clever salonnière in Paris had been obliged to marry her own daughter.

Don't laugh, said Grandmother Dummer, as she saw us burst out into giggles (for while we might like each other we certainly didn't want our harassed Mums as brides) – don't laugh, for it was the very same reason that drove Eve to marry Sally, not long after she'd found her and offered companionship in the lonely groves of Academe.

And the reason, of course, is competition. Just as that famous salonnière, whose name was Mme du Deffand, suggested marriage to her daughter as the only way of lessening the avid competition between them – for famous men, bright wits and fine conversation – so Eve quickly discovered that Sally, by now a budding Professor of Anthropology, was determined to be her deadly rival.

Oh, they lived together quite happily after the wedding ceremony, said Grandmother Dummer, and she laughed softly. But you must admit it's a fairly drastic course to have to take. Just because your husband is so jealous of you that he has actually been found at dead of night in the lab working on a poison so invisible in its traces that African pygmies have already placed an order – and because, too, your best woman friend has been as surely turned against you by that Divide-and-Rule policy which men have implemented so successfully down the centuries.

– And what did Eve ... and Sally wear? Elsie said, rather shyly I thought.

– For the wedding? Oh ... a veil of Brussels lace for Sally and a magnificent tiara for Eve. I must say, Grandmother Dummer added rather dreamily in her turn, Eve never looked more lovely than on that windy March day in a little University town.

Then, as if waking from a trance, Grandmother Dummer told us we mustn't on any account be put off developing our minds after her stories. For, of course, both Elsie and I dreamed of being at one of the great universities, in our mortarboards and gowns; and discovering a new Shakespeare play or learning how to decipher the code of the meaning of the universe.

As I was saying, said Grandmother Dummer, Adam feels threatened and left out. His original research on the sex life of the male sea-urchin turns out to be hopelessly out-dated; and anyway everyone is interested in Eve's line of business.

Which is precisely the meaning of life, the universe and everything. For Eve, after cracking DNA and the double helix (for which she received no recognition at all), has gone on to perfect cold nuclear fusion, thus supplying the world with a limitless amount of cheap electricity (but the big boys who run the nuclear reactors don't want to lose their profits, so they discredit her); now, last but not least, Eve has understood time and the working of atom particles that run backwards; so old wars can be mended and forests grow up again long after they have been sacrificed for the sake of a quick beefburger, and burnt down.

Oh, Eve has discovered how to save the world!

And it's true, says Grandmother Dummer, that Eve looked up at the great ozone hole gaping over our heads and she distinctly saw God's face there.

She knew by now which algebraic formulae described God and the meaning of the universe, and although she told all the bishops, and she demonstrated her theorem perfectly, so that on starry nights when Lilith was safely away blowing up her typhoons elsewhere, the heavens could be made, by a touch of Eve's pure mathematics, to open for an instant and the Divine Face was there –
– in spite of this, no one believed her.

Some said Eve had taken for herself the role of the Messiah and was pretending a Second Coming, as Ann Lee, the founder of the Shakers, a modest girl from Manchester, did two hundred years ago.

Others, who will always see Eve as the root of all temptation and sin, said they didn't know about coming for a second time when the first time had brought misfortune enough (they meant it as a sex joke, of course, and laughed so loud they forgot to look at the sky and see if their Heavenly Maker really was there after all).

*

Still others believed every word the popular press gave out about the millennial powers of the strange white-haired woman of the School of Night – as they called the college where once only the most classical experiments had been conducted.

These people thought the sky would fall in on them any minute. Like Henny Penny they scurried about, repeating the vulgar science of the tabloid press and understanding nothing of the meaning of Eve's unique scientific discovery.

– I may say, said Grandmother Dummer, as we scrambled down the path to the cove – and we saw she went more agilely than usual, as if the end of the day, and the end of the summer, were giving her strength somehow: as if she burned inside, with the telling of Eve's long journey from expulsion from Eden to neglect and contempt at the hands of men as little willing to grant her genius as the elders of the rabbinical sects had been to allow her a soul –

– I may say that Eve was a little disturbed by what she did see, sitting up there in the woolly clouds. After all that ... and Eve could be heard swearing to herself, in the thirteenth-century hermit's cell where the dons had locked her after her latest revelation of the divine truth through her revised quantum mechanics.

Well, blow me! Eve said – and worse, when she was let out on starry nights and stood in the quad and looked up at her Maker.

But Grandmother Dummer wouldn't tell us, however hard we pressed, what the face of God was actually like.

Eve might be disappointed, she said, but when our time came we might be perfectly happy with it. (This made us wonder if God wasn't after all a dear old man with a beard as white as the clouds, rather like Santa Claus; and although it was true we wouldn't mind this, we thought it was time the face of a beautiful black Eve looked down from up high – the first African mother goddess of us all.)

– However that may be, Grandmother Dummer said, Eve was soon disillusioned with the results of her scientific discoveries.

While men were greedy and determined to put profit before the future of the planet, the brilliance of astrophysicists such as Eve would be ignored and relegated to the wastepaper basket.

WITCH

– And Sally was getting on a bit, too, said Grandmother Dummer as she pulled off her wrap-around skirt and said she felt like one last plunge before the equinoctial gales came and blew the summer away.

So we decided to live together in a little cottage bought with the remains of Eve's salary as a professor – and some of Sally's money too, but we needn't enquire too closely as to where that came from.

We bought a cottage in that rocky piece of magic known as Cornwall ... and before long we had a reputation for being witches, you know.

– Well, what do you expect? Grandmother Dummer called out as she took the first stroke of her swim, and the water seemed to churn up a phosphorescent trail behind her.

If a woman isn't one type in the eyes of men, then she must be another.

*

– But … but … Elsie and I said. We stood on the shore: neither of us wanted to swim, for the wind was chilly, and we didn't like the shape of the rock out just in front of us, which in the half-light of evening, looked like a boat wrecked and overturned by the sheer power of the sea.

– Why – why 'we'? we said.

But we knew by now, I think. We remembered the children laughing and pointing at Grandmother Dummer when she went to the village for stores; and we remembered our indignation when a snotty little girl with acne and a white face from eating too many chocolate bars had told us that Grandmother Dummer was a big bad witch.

We understood slowly, as Grandmother Dummer turned to wave at us from far out to sea, that she was Elsie's grandmother Eve …

… and we learnt, as the mermaid on the rock, the mermaid of Zennor that had become a siren, sang her song of her journey through life to us, that we must try to change the world of men …

… and make a new Eve.